JACKFISH REBORN
BY REJEAN GIGUERE

Other books by Rejean Giguere

Raildogs
Endpoint
Franklin Asylum
Merlin 444
DreamWeaver

Short Story Collection

First Works

www.rejeangiguere.com
@rejeangiguere

JACKFISH REBORN

by Rejean Giguere

First Print Edition
Copyright 2013 - Rejean Giguere
ISBN 978-1-927047-20-0
Ontario, Canada
www.rejeangiguere.com

This book is a work of Fiction. All characters and events (and some places) are products of the Author's imagination.

JACKFISH THEN

Jackfish, Ontario 14/08/1939

Photo courtesy Terrace Bay Public Library

This book is dedicated to all the fans who have supported me so far on my journey to become a writer.

PROLOGUE

China, 2010

Chang "Dragon" Long sat across from his grand-mother. He couldn't understand the direction this conversation was taking. It seemed he was missing something.

His grandmother was one of those strong, intelligent women who helped advance a family's fortunes. In fact, he'd never known his great-grandfather who had disappeared in North America, so he'd received most of his wisdom from her. Now he could tell she was waiting patiently for him to catch up. Dragon stared down at the box of items that she had handed him. Apparently they were from his great-grandfather and she clearly wanted him to see them.

The odd assortment of papers meant nothing to him, but when she asked him to read it all again he knew he was supposed to find something. She was a smart one, and obviously she had a reason, so he went through the papers one last time trying to understand what was written there.

Some of the papers appeared to be contracts, and he understood some of the maps. They were all related to the businesses his family was involved in, drug running and mining.

Nothing stood out, but he was left with one piece of paper in his hand that he couldn't place. He knew it was the right one as he watched his grandmother smile.

The sheet of paper made no sense. It was like a riddle or a code;

Come to the land of tree and rock,
Simple people, land of riches, a fish named Jack.
Big tongue in the water, protected by two,
Walking steel eyes into the late day sun, past the two,
Leaving the ocean, finding the other side of three,
Wealth and prosperity, awaits in eights, the white lightning

He kept returning to the eights because he knew the number meant good luck. When he looked up, the confusion on his face clearly evident, his grandmother took a deep breath and leaned forward. "It is time eldest grandson. It is time to learn about your destiny."

Book 1
A Riddle

CHAPTER 1

China, 2012

Dragon Chang was twenty-four years old. Strong from years in the trade, he paced quietly along the mountain path. This would be his last trip leading the opium shipments from inside Burma to his home province of Yunnan, in southwest China. He would ensure the cargo made it from the jungle bases in Burma, where the processed opium originated, along the well-travelled routes through his territory, to the distributers in Macau.

His family had been associated with the TeoChiew, or TC triad, for generations. Relatives had even moved to Burma and Thailand to become part of that end of the supply chain. Years later the opium was constantly on the move. He used this route every third or fourth run, choosing from the many available trails along the fourteen hundred miles of border between China and Burma.

Dragon stopped suddenly. His eyes squinted as he strained to hear something. Impossible to most people, he had an ability to hear in the rain and to sense the unexpected. Now he stood there with his eyes closed and let his flexing muscles transmit the threat which had brought him to a halt.

The two men travelling with him ahead of the mule train had used this route many times and knew the land well. Dragon turned to the first one. "Return to the train, get it off the trail until we come back for you."

There was no answer as the man hurried back to meet the cargo.

To the other he said, "The valley opens up close to here, we'll find high ground."

Dragon headed off the trail towards a rising hill. In the west of the province it was all steep hills and valleys running north and south. It was beautiful unless you had to climb the hills. Today their route worked its way up a canyon beside a raging river. He knew that this side of the valley would give him a clear view of the trail that wound its way along the other side.

Intensity mixed with the rain on his face, not from the fear of what might be ahead, but in anticipation of what was to come.

Who would make the mistake of hitting one of his trains? These guys weren't the first ones to try, but like others before them, their first attempt would be the last.

This was Dragon's last shipment. It had taken him over a year to convince his father to let him follow his dream and take his place in expanding the family business.

For generations the family had followed the same pattern. One generation kept the supply routes running and promoted their legitimate businesses. The next generation spread out to new territory, expanding the family fortunes.

Dragon's father was very influential, he hardly ever saw the man who was constantly on the move in the mountains while running the trade. His father's generation the one entrusted to stay in the mountains, keeping routes open, keeping things flowing. He knew his father took this responsibility seriously and was doing whatever was required to keep the family fortune protected.

It was his father who showed him the routes and introduced him to their contacts. He'd also been the first to show Dragon the lengths required to protect the family business.

The memory of these brutal lessons brought him back to his immediate concern. His anger was inching closer to the surface, and he hadn't even seen the danger yet. It might just be simple peasant women out on a supply run. Still, he ground his teeth at the thought it could be something else.

Dragon had grown up exercising a level of power, even when he was young he could tell his family was dangerous. He himself had never been weakened by fear, but excelled at creating it in others. He wrinkled his nose in disgust at the thought and shook the rain off his head momentarily. After climbing twenty yards up the hill, he got down and crawled the last ten feet to a ledge where he could look down into the valley. The other man crawled up beside him.

He was sure someone was out there, coming up the trail. His instincts had never been wrong before. He was patient, which was something he didn't learn from his father, but from his grandmother. It had been two years since the day she had given him his great-grandfather's papers and explained that she didn't think the old man had died in vain.

Chang "Tiger" Cheng was supposed to expand the family, and had taken advantage of an opportunity to sail the far seas. He had ended up in Canada at a time it was a virgin land that had hardly been explored. It had always been assumed that Tiger died there sometime around 1885. The cryptic riddle in his final letters home had contained references to wealth and prosperity, but had meant nothing to anyone in the family.

His grandmother reminded him that he had an obligation to move away and expand the family business.

Suddenly, a nudge from his partner made Dragon dial in on what was going on down in the valley. It took a moment to find them through the falling rain and drifting fog that hung between the mountains. Once he spotted them he went completely still, staring like a hawk. The outlines of four strangers walked up and over a knoll before their trail disappeared back behind a large bank of rock.

He closed his eyes briefly, enjoying the feel of adrenaline working its way into his system. It was his only drug. He waited for the intruders to cross a larger open area. A slight smile spread across his face.

Now that they were out in the open and he was sure they were alone, he thought to himself, four of you, that's a bad number, it means death. Two of us is a good number, good things come in pairs. He smiled widely. "Li, we'll take them out from here."

From this distance he wasn't really sure who they were. They could be soldiers, police, or another gang. Either way, it wasn't someone who ruled in this area, because that fell to him and his family. Dragon took the bag off his shoulder and hunched over to create a rain-stop while he unloaded the M99 sniper rifle. His father always believed in having the right equipment for the job. Even though the family looked like struggling miners to everyone else, they were highly efficient and deadly in the mountains. One thing they never had was a shortage of money and connections.

The rifle was more than he really needed, the fifty-calibre bullets could punch holes through armoured vests. He settled over the stock, feeling the wet metal against his jaw. He knew how far it was across the valley and adjusted the scope slightly. Aiming at the next knoll along the trail he waited for them to appear.

How many times had he fought in these hills? It was personal to him that he was successful on his last run, and it pissed him off that these intruders were even here. It was time though, he looked through the scope entering into another world.

Everything around him evaporated, he stopped listening and let his eye take over. The path was enlarged in the scope. He was always amazed at the distance you could kill from. He was picking out the individual pebbles on the trail when he saw the first figure step out into the open.

The sight of combat fatigues was enough, and Dragon flipped off the safety, still watching through the scope. He let the first two men cross his field of view and waited for the third one to appear. The third one was his first target. Surprise was everything. Taking the rain into account, he gently pulled the trigger. A slight correction and he was onto number two who had almost made his way across the opening. He pulled the trigger a second time.

The two cracks of the rifle could be heard through the rain, and the remaining men scattered. The first guy went forward, the last one went back, spreading them apart. His two kills were laid out like broken rag dolls on the trail. Dragon's eye never left the scope, he swung back towards the last knoll the intruders had crossed and waited. On cue, his next victim peeked out from behind the top of the knoll before trying to retreat across the open space.

Dragon had been waiting for that move and the trigger moved slightly. The man wasn't any better off than his buddies, the round slammed him sideways and he landed in a heap. Lowering the rifle, he stood up and relaxed slightly. "Li, you take the last one and get the bodies off the trail. I'll get the train."

*****

The Chinese gangster went to ground when the first rifle shots rang out. He was in someone else's territory. They had known that, and been prepared to negotiate an arrangement with whoever ran this area in order to smuggle drugs from Burma. Obviously these people weren't interested and now two of his comrades were dead.

Another shot let him know that his third friend had indeed tried to run back down the trail. He was terrified. He had to stay hidden, but had to get moving. Looking around he crawled up to a rock ledge that was between him and the shooter, turning to stand with his back against it. He didn't get much time to think.

The figure dropping onto the trail from above, landed in front of him. A machete sliced into his shoulder on the way past, driving him to the ground with the force of the blow. Looking up, he could see arms holding the blade, everything else was blocked out. There was only a silhouette of the man in the pouring rain. All he was able to focus on were the tattoos running up the two arms as they jerked the blade free.

He held back a scream, even with his arm hanging away from his body. But as he was grabbed and dragged to the river's edge he began to yell. His only thought as his screams hit the rushing water was that he'd never learnt to swim.

*****

Dragon's pack train continued along the ancient trail until they came to one of the changeover camps. Here the bundles were unloaded from the mules and transferred into small vehicles. They would make their way overland through Guangxi and Guangdong provinces towards the chaos of Macau.

Dragon had been to the end of the route a number of times back when he began his training. His father wanted him to see the product all the way to the docks and the ships that would take it away. He usually turned around here with the mules and let his men take it the rest of the way. The load was secure and the most dangerous part was over now that the product was moving in vehicles.

He thought back to his first runs. He could laugh at it now. How their connections must have looked at him as he came down the trail with one bundle and one mule. Dragon had thought he was a major player while his father had let him get his footing.

Now the trains were huge, this one had twenty mules and one hundred bundles. It would take three vehicles to carry it all.

This shipment alone would generate huge profits. Paying the farmer one thousand for the raw opium, they would refine the product and move it to North America where it sold for one hundred and fifty thousand. Even he realized this was an exceptional return.

This time Dragon would be riding with these bundles to the end of the line. He was going to the docks with his right hand man Li. They would catch a ride on one of the ships and pursue the dream his great-grandfather had begun.

It was hard to leave these hills and the comforts of family. Bouncing along the small goat paths in one of the vehicles, Dragon thought about his great-grandfather's riddle. He had spent a lot of time turning it over in his head, in doing as much research as he could. In the end he knew he would have to trace his great-grandfather's travels to piece it together.

It was when Dragon studied the construction route of the Canadian Pacific Railroad where the family assumed his great-grandfather had died, that he hit the jackpot. A ghost town along the north shore of Lake Superior called Jackfish. It was a long shot that this was the fish named Jack at the beginning of the riddle, but he was going to have to start somewhere.

This intrigued Dragon the most. If his hunch was correct, then Tiger left them clues to a place that was now a ghost town. What did that mean? Was there any significance? He was putting a lot of faith in this place Jackfish.

He couldn't figure out anything else from the riddle his grandmother had given him, but it seemed that this was the place to start. Dragon knew he was really just a mountain miner and part-time gangster. Even with his piles of money, he was unfamiliar with the rest of the world. This trip to another continent was going to take all the skill and courage he had. He looked at Li sitting beside him and smiled. He'd need all the muscle he could get.

CHAPTER 2

Hours later the small convoy crawled towards the populated section of the coast along the South China Sea. Soon they were crossing the bridge over the Xi river, turning off the highway towards the hustle of the tight streets and bright lights of Macau. Compared to his place in the mountains Dragon loved this city. He had to sacrifice the comfort he found in the silence of the mountain nights, but was excited by the noise and nightlife of the city.

The small convoy headed down Shihua East Road towards the container port. Circling around the freight and customs warehouses, his driver pulled up to the back gate of the trucking yard where the triad controlled things. Waved through quickly, the cars headed along the busy docks to a ship anchored near the end. Without many words the deck hands and smugglers began hauling the bundles up the gangway. This ship was bound for Vancouver in the morning. Dragon and Li were going on a second freighter also leaving the next day. That gave the men some time to enjoy a bit of the nightlife.

Dragon had to be careful. As much as he ruled his area of the mountains, and he would be welcome in any TC Triad's bar or restaurant, Macau was a major centre for distribution, prostitution and gambling. The other triads were active here as well. He would have to make sure he didn't cross any hidden boundaries.

He felt a huge weight on his shoulders. Would he make it back to China, or was he leaving for the first and last time? Once their product was loaded onto the ship they all piled into the vehicles and headed out to get drunk.

The bar was just a few steps off the trendy Sun Yat Sen Avenue. The dark and run down exterior of the gang hangout of local TC Triad members was a hundred years apart from the imitation Miami dance clubs lining the avenue. Dragon was enjoying his beer and unwinding a little. The life of a drug runner was intense and he had spent the last couple weeks in a heightened state of alert.

Li sat beside him. Close calls and scrapes had brought them close. Li's family had worked for his since before both of them were born. Dragon looked at him as an equal and as a friend.

He lifted his beer. "Our last run together Li. May our luck be as good in the new world."

"Cheers to the new world." Li tipped his beer in salute.

His answer wasn't that enthusiastic. All along Dragon's planning assumed that Li would want to come. Now he wondered if he had it wrong. "You don't sound that excited Li. You don't have to take this trip if it doesn't suit you."

"It's the uncertainty of the trip. I'm not sure where we are going or what we are trying to do." Li took a drink from his beer, "besides when will we see a smooth Chinese woman again?"

Dragon burst out laughing. "That is all you ever think of, but you do raise a serious issue." Dragon hadn't thought about it, and the way Li said it really got him thinking. "Maybe we better find some girls tonight Li, it could be our last chance."

He waved over their local connection, who had brought them to the bar, instructing him to take them where they could find some women. The five men ended up in the red-light end of town outside a strip club. Dragon let his contact do the talking at the door, then followed him inside.

The interior was a stark contrast to the rundown neon-lit exterior. Inside flashing strobe lights swirled, casting beams through the cigarette smoke. Dragon felt the bass of the music punch against his chest as if he had run into a wall.

Li stopped, just staring. There were more naked women that either of them had ever seen in one place before. On the stage, carrying drinks, dancing in front of men at their tables, the gorgeous women were clearly available for a good time.

Dragon noticed curtained booths set off to one side. He let their contact know he wanted one of those, where he could have more privacy and less scrutiny. Once a little money changed hands they were inside their own space.

When the first waitress came in to take their orders, Dragon pulled her aside, "Can you get seven or eight women to join us for the night." He flashed some of the money he had tucked into his inner jacket. "Girls who want to have fun," he said with a smile.

Soon the little curtained booth was rocking. He threw some money down on the table, welcoming the women for the evening. The dancers were ecstatic as they divvied up their shares of more money than they might ordinarily earn in a month, settling in to have some fun.

Dragon watched over the scene for a bit as Li and the three other men indulged themselves with the naked women. Never shy in public, Li wasted no time, and quickly was thrusting himself into a woman in the corner.

Once word got around the bar about the generous flow of money, other women approached, asking if they could join the party. Over the next hour Dragon stayed alert and ensured the other men had their fun.

When he could tell Li was finally done with his third woman, he settled back to enjoy himself. Two of their local contacts were leaving, one staying behind to keep him and Li company. Dragon let a few new girls into the booth and encouraged the rest of the others to leave. He wanted it a little less crowded.

Finally he leaned back against the booth and pointed at his lap. One of the women straddled his legs, facing him. He felt his pants open and the zipper go down. She reached in and pulled him out.

Dragon looked her in the eye as she stroked him. Rising up, she held his gaze as she moved closer, dropping down, taking him all at once. He leaned his head back and let the woman move on him. She closed her eyes, slowly sliding up and down.

When a menacing looking young gangster suddenly burst through the curtain, Li jumped up to confront him. The woman on top of Dragon froze momentarily, until he put his hands on her waist and started her moving slowly again.

"Li, wait." Dragon's voice was calm. He could see the intruder clearly from his position and knew he was a threat. "Who the fuck are you?"

That seemed to have caught the young man off guard, he'd probably expected the men to fear him, but it was obvious they didn't.

"Who the fuck am I? Who the fuck, are you?" The gangster took a few steps forward, vibrating with anger. He couldn't believe the balls of this guy, who just kept the woman going up and down as if he wasn't concerned at all. "You got yourself a serious problem here and you don't even understand it."

The gangster kept his right arm turned forward like he wanted them to see his 14K triad tattoo. He obviously wanted them to know that he was beyond the reach of police and the authorities. He seemed to think he could do whatever he wanted.

Dragon had two choices. Let Li make quick work of the guy, which would mean they would have to fight their way out. Or, he could use the negotiating skills his father had taught him and the patience his grandmother had taken the time to instil in him.

He wanted, without a doubt, to mess this asshole up. It would have been a sure thing if they were in the mountains, but one did have to adjust in the city. He looked at the woman who had started to speed up her movements and again used his hands to slow her down.

Raising his right hand, he pointed at the young gangster. "You better get your boss, because you've made a big mistake."

Now the guy was losing his momentum, bosses meant upper-level triad members, and he obviously wasn't anywhere near that point yet. Dragon watched him struggle with the thought that this might be a friend of his bosses and perhaps he was in over his head. He could see the moment when the young gangster decided he wasn't letting it go, he'd heard about the money floating around and was going to get some if these guys weren't protected.

"I'll get my boss asshole, just so he can watch me screw you guys up."

Dragon never even looked up. He was starting to really enjoy the woman's movements and kept his focus on her. "We'll be waiting I'm sure. Now go get someone boy." He knew that would really piss the kid off. After all, Dragon wasn't much older than he was, but he continued to ignore him as he steamed out of the booth.

"Okay woman, it's time." Finally he let her speed up, rising higher and higher until she brought him to a satisfying release. That was the way he wanted to remember his women. He had business to deal with now and he quickly lifted her off his lap and pointed to the door. She seemed relieved to get out of there, he was sure she knew the shit was coming.

Street level gangsters were at each other constantly, fighting for space, but he also knew that the triads operated together at the highest levels to ensure everything ran smoothly. He would let that be his card out of here. "Li, calm is required. I will let you know if I need your help."

The curtain flew open a second time and in walked the young gangster with one of his bosses. This one was older and rounder, and moved with purpose. He was covered in tattoos, his 14K symbol out in the open. He looked briefly at Li before settling on Dragon. "This is the man you speak of? Where is the woman he used while he threatened you?"

"She was here," was all the youngster replied.

The boss continued to stare at Dragon. "You bring trouble to one of my bars? And to one of my men?"

"I came in to enjoy some liquor and women. We took a booth to be private and considerate to the other patrons. This useless man of yours interrupted us and has been rude and insulting." Dragon stood up and faced the older gangster head on. "Which I hold against you. The question is, will this end here, or is it going to escalate?" Dragon took off his coat and rolled up his sleeves. He made sure his own tattoo was clearly visible.

All tattoos said something to those who knew what to look for. The gangster would see the TeoChiew triad symbol represented by the TC, but it was the symbol above it that would get his attention.

Anyone affiliated with the triads had a symbol saying so. If the symbol was below the triad tattoo, it meant that they were under the triads control and reported to them. If it was beside the triad tattoo, it meant that they were in partnership with the triad, as equals.

When the symbol was above the triad tattoo, like Dragon's, it meant the person was integral to the triad's profits and highly respected. Someone that was to be protected at all times. Dragon watched the gangster as he put it together.

The man could still take a shot at them. He was a gangster from another triad and might get away with it; but he'd be wondering if it was allowed. Look at the mistake his soldier had already made.

The man was in an uncomfortable position, he couldn't believe this young tough-looking kid was attached to the higher levels. It was all about saving face now. "My apologies for the rudeness of a simple soldier. We will leave you to your evening."

"Just make sure that there are no more incidents tonight," Dragon let that hang a second. "Are we clear?"

The gangster nodded as he pushed his soldier out through the curtain. Dragon and Li had another drink and decided they needed to get out of there. Their contact, who had been quiet and uninvolved through the entire hassle, was still with them. He was providing a bed to stay that night, so the three of them left the club, heading for his place.

The contact took two steps onto the sidewalk before he was swarmed. *Shit*, Dragon had known it was still a possibility. If that boss was a hothead he might have been embarrassed and wanting to do something about it. As long as his bosses didn't find out, there would be no consequences.

Big mistake. The gangster should have been worrying about Dragon's group instead of his own bosses. As their contact went down, Li jumped forward. He pulled his machete from the back sling hidden under his coat and went to work.

Swinging the deadly blade in an X pattern in front of him, Li walked into the group, taking off outstretched arms or legs as they presented themselves. Dragon looked at faces until he found the boss he had spoken to. He could see the man was shocked at the sudden explosion of flying body parts as Li began to wreak havoc. The man started to back up, separating himself from the group.

Dragon surged towards the boss who saw him coming at the last second. As the man tried to maneuver out of the way, he was hit hard and driven backwards onto the ground. Dragon landed hard on top of him and quickly gained the upper hand. Now he had the gangster pinned.

He took a quick moment to turn and check the others. Their contact was getting up off the pavement and there wasn't a group of attackers left. Those uninjured by Li's initial assault were running in every direction. The rest were screaming, crawling or stumbling away from the viscous attack.

Dragon looked down at the gangster again and made sure the man saw the anger on his face.

"You've made a mistake Mr. Big Boss, and now you are going to pay."

Before the gangster had a chance to wonder what was coming, Dragon drove his head downward, smashing it into the guy's face. There was an awful crack. He pulled back and watched the face explode with blood from a broken nose that was now bent over to the left.

"You'll have a memory of this night forever."

The boss was struggling to breathe as the blood running down the back of this throat was starting to make him cough. Dragon slammed his head down again, making sure he connected forehead to forehead. He cut himself in the process, as he battered the gangster, causing the skin above the man's eye to flap open.

"Every time you see the scars in the mirror, or someone asks about them, I am sure you will lie and tell a story; but deep inside you will know you are a piece of shit who was beaten like an old woman."

The gangster was close to passing out from the second blow. He tried to focus his eyes through the blood and pick out his attacker's face. Dragon drove his head down a third time, connecting with the man's jaw. The eerie noise caused him to look down to see the man's jawbone had shifted to one side.

Dragon jumped to his feet. "We're out of here. We don't need any more problems tonight."

The three men stepped over the bodies littering the road and started to run down the street. Dragon was feeling the booze, laughing as he remembered the fight and the woman. Tomorrow was the eighth of the month, the number eight was a good omen and good luck. He felt the energy roaring through his veins and he looked over at Li as they ran. "China – why would we ever leave?"

CHAPTER 3

Marathon, Ontario, Canada. East of Jackfish, 1883

"The ground is alive. It eats the rail overnight."

The worker's comment rang true. Tiger couldn't believe it himself. They would lay track one day and the earth would devour it by the next. If it wasn't the rain and rivers washing it away, the steel simply sank below the surface.

This was the mess he was in. Somewhere near a town that would eventually be called Marathon, in Canada's north. The delays didn't stop the madness though, the men continued laying the rails that were supposed to link this massive land. They blasted and moved rock, levelling the mountains, filling the swamps and flattening the valleys to keep the track level.

He and the other Chinese workers were kept away from the locals. They camped together in tents, working ahead of the main crews, doing the most dangerous work. Tiger didn't mind, it worked in his favor.

He didn't know how long his family had been in the crime business, but it went way back. His father had worked poppy routes, affiliated with the triads like previous generations.

Tiger thought he had it made and had settled down with a nice bride, only to have the family history of "secure and expand" explained to him. This was the way that the Chang family would continue to grow and prosper. His destiny was to spread the family's influence by moving to another country. He picked North America based on talks he'd had with ship captains. They said the place was, "a country the size of China with no one living there. A place full of mountains, rivers, and endless wilderness."

Well, he had sure found the wilderness endless. For over a year he had been working this rail, and he couldn't believe how big the country was. They had been laboring along the north side of a large lake called Superior for over four months now. Whenever they climbed a hill with enough height that they could see the big water, Tiger always took the time to sit and ponder its size.

"This is just a lake Bao, can you believe it?"

His trusted lieutenant was equally amazed by its size. "They say that there are other lakes to the south just as big."

Tiger nodded, he really wanted to get off the damned railroad and get on with the family business. He almost left a few times, but kept working the next section. Right now he had too much going his way here in the middle of nowhere.

He had been in Canada a year before they started bringing laborers from China to work as crews on the railroad. He'd been quick to see an opportunity. When the first crews arrived in the eastern province to start working westward, he was in place and quickly found ways to put himself in an influential position.

Finding some men who were not leaders, but who liked the respect they received as feared soldiers, he quickly organized them into a group. Hearing that Chinese workers were getting beat up on nights when drunken local men were wandering around looking for trouble was the opportunity he was seeking. This would be where he gained the trust of his people.

*****

The fire had been stoked with large logs up to a foot wide. The flames jumped high into the night air, creating a bright, warm circle in the cold dark night. The Chinese workers were laughing and getting drunk. Tiger and his men watched from the woods surrounding the clearing.

On one hand his men should be sleeping and getting the rest needed to just survive the heavy work. On the other hand, he could understand their desire to unwind and escape the harshness of a backbreaking job. As long as they worked the next day, he had no issues.

Tiger hoped that this weekend would bring them the trouble he was looking for. He was getting tired of listening to his own men getting drunk and carrying on, if the locals didn't show up soon he was going to do something to somebody, one way or the other.

After two hours huddled in the cold dark inside the tree line, they heard people coming through the woods towards the fire. He silently waved his men down, low to the ground.

"Come on guys, they're over here!"

The *gwei lo*, white devils, were making just as much noise as the celebrating Chinese, egging each other on. It seemed they were trying to keep their courage up.

"Let's get in there before they try to run."

A short loudmouth led three tough looking men into the opening. Tiger watched the drinking workers jump up and move to the other side of the fire, clumping up like a herd of scared sheep. Not one of them moved forward to confront the intruders.

The smallest white man was first to speak. "Well, what have we got here? Looks like a bunch of little boys all huddled together."

The three big guys laughed and started flexing their muscles, trying to look tough. One of them punched his fist into his palm a few times which seemed to intimidate the intoxicated Chinese.

Tiger could see the intoxicated workers were clearly not interested in defending themselves, which was fine with him. He'd hoped they wouldn't.

Without a word, he got up and stepped into the clearing. Bao and three others ranged out beside him. In a line they walked towards the locals. The intruders heard the murmurs of the Chinese huddled on the other side of the fire and turned to see Tiger and his group. Initially, the white men didn't see any difference between these Chinese and those on the other side of the flames. Then they caught the glint of a knife and heard the unmistakable sound of metal on metal as a machete was pulled from it's sheathe.

The three big men lost a bit of their courage at the sight of the unknown arrivals, these clearly weren't the pushovers they were looking for, but the smallest one was still cocky. "Look here boys, we got us some Chinamen with balls." His smile looked like a snarl.

Tiger knew this was his intended target. "So you think it is fun to beat up on men from my country. Well here I am." He spread his hands open in from of him as he moved towards the smaller man. "Let's have some fun."

Tiger watched the sudden spike of fear as the gang's leader looked around at his men for help.

"Are you not man enough to fight your own battles?" The question brought laughter from Tiger's own group and some of the drunken men around the fire who could understand English.

The fear started to change to anger in the eyes of the other man. He was being called out in front of witnesses. He appeared to be calculating his odds and trying to gauge the difficulties this Chinese was going to bring.

Tiger stepped closer as everyone else moved away. His men backed up while the three big men, unsure what to do, created some separation from their boss.

Fighting was something that Tiger had learned in the mountains protecting the family's smuggling routes. The only way to fight was to stay on the offensive and be as brutal as possible. As he lunged forward, the white man tried to move away. Tiger hit him square in the chest and kept pushing backwards. He didn't care what they hit or fell on, just that the local was below him.

Tiger kept pushing the man, warding off his blows until they slammed up against a tree. As the air rushed out of his opponent's lungs, he pulled him away from the tree and threw him towards the fire. The man landed on his side and rolled a few times before coming to a stop dangerously close to the flames. He quickly tried to lever himself up out of the dirt, but Tiger was already beside him, kicking him hard in the ribs.

Now all the intoxicated Chinese were yelling and cheering, excited to see the local being beaten. The three tough guys weren't running away, but they weren't hurrying to their leader's defence either. The man curled up in a defensive position as Tiger kicked him in the side again, he was sure he felt ribs give way.

He leaned over his victim. "You mentioned a bunch of boys. I only see one here." Reaching down he grabbed the man's arm, stretching it towards the fire. Sliding his hands back to the guy's elbow, Tiger thrust the hand into the heat.

He'd expected his victim's sudden struggle to pull the hand out of the fire and braced himself, keeping the hand against the coals for a few moments. Stepping back Tiger let go of the man's arm and the leader jerked it out of the fire, staring in shock at his melted flesh.

"You can't do that!" One of the big tough guys found his courage.

Tiger ignored him. He turned to his countrymen still huddled on the other side of the fire. "What's wrong with you? Have you no pride in yourself or your country?" He asked in Chinese.

Again, there were murmurs in the drunken crowd.

"You are scared of men like this?" He kicked the contorted man on the ground. "You cannot let this happen, or you will be slaves in this country. Stand up for yourselves and protect your own."

Tiger turned and nodded. His lieutenant jumped forward, straight into the big man who had finally stepped out to protect his boss. Bao swung his machete, aiming the back side of the blade for the big man's knee. Everyone in the clearing heard the impact as the man's leg buckled and he toppled over sideways, landing on his back.

An overhead swing, still using the back of the blade, came down hard on the other leg just missing the knee.

"Jesus Christ," the man yelled as he jerked upright, trying to protect his legs with his arms.

Bao brought the butt end of the machete down on the man's head, the hardened steel splitting his scalp open, the force of the blow flattening him back out on the ground.

"Look what a Chinese can do!" Tiger yelled at his countrymen who were getting more enraged and vocal.

"I took one man. Bao here took down this big one by himself." He let his voice go quiet as everyone listened. "Can't you men take care of these other two by yourselves?" He swung his arm around to indicate the remaining tough guys.

The crowd started to yell, moving together around the fire pit.

The two tough guys hadn't understood the conversation, but could tell things had taken a bad turn. They started to back up, trying to retreat. The crowd surged from behind the fire and spread out, surrounding the men.

Tiger, Bao, and his men stood back and let the mob go. Blows rained down and the mass of men surrounding the tough guys kept beating until the men had fallen, huddling on the ground in self-defence. Tiger led his group away, certain that his reputation had been established and that word would spread throughout the rest of the Chinese workers.

*****

There were twelve thousand men and five thousand horses working out of the makeshift town at Marathon. The five hundred Chinese workers were no longer having any problems with the locals. They were left alone and kept to themselves.

Tiger had strengthened his grip on the Chinese workers by getting supplies, better food rations, providing protection, and then strong-arming them all for small payments to keep things running smoothly. He became the go-between for the workers and the railroad's big bosses.

The last thing he did cemented his leadership and gave him complete control. He managed to get the bosses off the work-site. Management showed up for morning and evening inspections, but otherwise the Chinese were left alone to get their work done.

When Tiger introduced a system where twenty different workers were excused from the work detail each day to rest, their appreciation multiplied as did their health and the crew's moral. Each day a handful of men were sent to hide and rest in the woods, out of sight in case someone came by.

As Tiger walked along the rail inspecting the work in progress, he turned to Bao. "Why are we still on this damned railroad?"

"Because it is profitable." The answer was simple, but exact. Tiger was putting away a nice sum every month, as were his soldiers.

"Yes, but isn't this living in hell out here? I'm sick of it."

"They say that they will put it a siding forty miles ahead at a place that they are calling Jackfish. There will be room for better accommodations and we will work from that camp for a period of time."

Tiger was silent while Bao continued, "Maybe we should wait until then, things may be better there."

He'd heard it before, the next place, the next place. That carrot was working well. He would continue to this new place and decide what to do once he got there. Tiger yelled down at a group of workers carrying rocks down into a hole that required filling. The fools couldn't even do a simple task.

He didn't work hard himself, but his presence was always felt as he did the organization and planning, or strong-arming as required. With his men as crew leaders directing the workers and Bao at his side, Tiger was now the uncontested leader.

CHAPTER 4

Jackfish, 2012

The man stood on the north shore of Lake Superior, swaying in the wind like the trees that surrounded him. He could be seen there if anyone had looked. But that was what was perfect about this place, there was no one looking.

The beard had grown in, offering protection against the elements. His hair had long gone unruly, whipping around on its own as the wind buffeted him. The clouds were rolling in and the fall breezes were getting cold. Phil Hardy flinched and rolled his shoulders in an effort to get rid of the chill.

"Jesus, you're getting cold these days," he said to the lake.

Since coming to this place a beaten man he had found comfort staring out at the water. He couldn't tell you why, but the breaking waves lapping against the shore chipped away at the anger and the pain.

Tearing himself away from the water, he climbed up the trail from the beach, brushing aside the moss hanging from the spruce trees as he headed towards the railway line. He had traps to check today and that singular task was all he was going to focus on. His family had been in this neck of the woods at one time and had known about a piece of property. It had taken some wrangling and negotiation, but he'd finally been able to secure it for himself.

The fifty acres acted like a backdrop to the old ghost town of Jackfish. The two large granite outcrops on Phil's property boxed the town in between the train tracks and the lake. The only regular activity these days came from the railroaders who used the siding east of town to work on the trains.

Whenever he came down off the hill where he'd put up a shelter, it was easier to use the tracks to get around instead of crashing through the forest or climbing over the hills. He'd only been into the nearest town a handful of times, so he assumed it was the train conductors who knew he was in the area and that was pretty much it.

What a contrast, the spiral from hell he'd escaped in the gray city to the green of the wilderness, and the salvation he was finding in this landscape. He stopped and stood still again. Squinting down the clear-cut of the rail line he thought he saw something. He'd found he was prone to stopping like that and just letting his senses take over.

Phil had put his watch away eight months ago when he left the city and came north. Now time stood still and he liked it that way. He didn't have a lot of goals. Just to live and survive on his own. He didn't figure it was a good idea to be around people these days and welcomed the isolation.

He started walking farther up the tracks, heading into the wind with the advantage if anything was up there. The trap-line he'd set out was illegal, he just didn't care. Phil was having a hard time these days with rules. Hell, anything to do with bureaucracy would get him going. As much as being alone in the woods might be helping him, it had the side benefit of keeping everyone else safe.

He stood there with his eyes closed and his head cocked slightly to the side.

He whispered into the wind. "Who's out there?"

He could hear things a lot better these days, the quiet was an incredible improvement. It had taken weeks to get the sounds of the city out of his head. In the beginning he'd hear blaring sirens and ringing phones while he tried to sit in peace on top of the hill staring out over the water. Now all he heard was the wilderness.

He turned his nose into the wind and sifted through the scents in the air. He could smell nature, but couldn't identify everything, he knew this sense should improve like the others. It was just a matter of time. Phil looked back down the track. *Nothing there.* Turning his head slowly back to the front, he cracked his neck to one side then the other, took a quick look up at the increasing clouds and started walking again.

"Okay, don't show yourself."

The old thirty-ought-six rifle slung over his shoulder was a comfort in these parts. Dressed in camouflage and prospector hiking boots, he wanted to blend in as much as possible. Phil had no illusions about the danger out here. He had moved onto their turf after all.

It used to be just moose this far up north, but climate change meant the deer were starting to become more common. It didn't matter. It was bear, wolf and cougar that he was watching for. Every place had their big three, and those were his. There was one big bear and a few smaller ones in the area. He'd seen them often enough.

Sitting up on the hill in the evening he'd watch down the tracks for a long distance. That was how he'd seen the large wolf. From the tracks he'd found he knew that it must come through on a somewhat regular basis.

He stopped again on the railroad tracks and let the place move around him. When he was sure it was clear, he continued. What concerned Phil the most was the cougar. He hadn't seen it yet, but it was leaving the most prints around for him to find, and that pointed to the predator living nearby.

He heard a voice somewhere in the back of his head. *Here kitty, kitty.*

Twenty minutes later he came to a flat opening covered in waist-high brush. He had set his snares around the field, and should have a rabbit or two if he was lucky. He stared at the thicket for a minute on full alert. Comfortable that nothing was off, he slowly made his way towards the forest that framed the open field.

Walking along the edge of the trees he watched the ground as he placed each foot. He listened and scanned his eyes quickly from side to side. He didn't push through branches and let them whip back making noise, he held them and walked through, then released them slowly

It didn't matter what your job was, you needed to focus. Phil's eyes wanted to jerk and look at each shadow and branch shifting in the wind, but he kept his eyes ahead and kept himself aware. If he started turning left and right, staring into the woods, then something could come at him from the opposite side.

No, Phil kept his eyes ahead and trusted that he'd know if something was real or not. It wasn't any different than being in a crowded condo building and not knowing if the tenants were gang-bangers or innocents. You had to wait until they acted.

The first snare was a kill. Phil stared down at the dead rabbit. He didn't like to kill anything, but had made that choice when he moved off the grid. He was doing it the hard way, the old way. The simple slip-noose had been hung on the edge of the bush, just off the ground. The rabbit looked like a good-sized adult.

"Well, you'll do just fine."

Within minutes he had the noose reset, the kill over his shoulder and was walking along the tree line again. He stopped suddenly, this time instinctively.

"Whoa there buddy."

Something was there, he could feel it. He looked down quickly at the second trap, confirming he had another one, which meant a good day. Unless you were a rabbit.

With two kills over his shoulder, Phil wanted to get to the next trap which was nearby. Silently he reached behind himself and brought the rifle around, making sure it was ready. Stepping quietly, trying not to break any fallen branches, creating noise. He covered the seven steps to the next bush.

Shit. Something had eaten the rabbit. The fur was mostly blown away but a few bones were strewn across the ground with the mangled noose. He looked around quickly and decided what to do. There was only one trap left, and it was on the other side of the opening. He'd leave that one today and just back out of the clearing and head home with the two he had.

Patience was something he'd lost completely before coming north. Out here it could be the difference between life and death. The safest thing to do was backtrack out the same way he'd come in. He was sure whatever it was, was still ahead of him, retreating was logical.

In the worst-case scenario he was being followed, and would walk right into something.

Finally out on the rail-line Phil felt a little more at ease. It was late in the afternoon and looked like it might rain, but he felt better walking along the rails. He checked behind him a few times to make sure he wasn't being followed. When he went to leave the tracks and start down to the beach he looked back one last time.

Phil froze. Something was standing on the tracks a quarter mile away, near the open area he had just left. He was glad the wind was blowing his way and he stood there trying to figure out what kind of animal it was. After he watched it for a moment he was sure it was a bear. It seemed to be heading the other way.

"Yes, you keep right on going." He reminded himself to always listen to that instinct.

The rabbits needed to be cleaned and he always did that on the shore. The mess might get washed away or blown into the water. Eagles and gulls would find the remains quickly. He skinned the animal and cut away everything but the meat.

He wouldn't have wanted to see his own snarl as he used the knife.

*****

The top of the two big hills provided a two hundred and ten degree view of the water from about eight or nine stories up.

The eastern-most hill had a channel of rock cut away where the train ran parallel to Lake Superior.

Along the north shore of Superior the rail line was boxed in between the water and the granite hills of the Canadian Shield. Where the hills came down to the water's edge the crews blasted level cuts in the rock just wide enough for a train, leaving the rail line framed by shear granite cliffs on either side, sometimes five or ten stories high. In this case the first hill was too big to go around and boxed in by the water, they'd had no choice but to go straight through the edge of it. The cliff it created here was a straight drop down to the track. Phil picked this hill to live on.

Christ, what a view, was all he'd been able to say the first time he climbed it.

The climb to the top was no simple task, but settling in was work he dug into and enjoyed as he began his new life. His biggest problem was getting the supplies and water for cement up to the top of the hill where he built an enclosure with steel posts and heavy fencing.

The second hardest job had been cutting the half-mile long trail that meandered through the thick forest and over the exposed granite rock to get to the top. He didn't need a lot, in fact didn't want a lot. The small solar panel and a bottle of propane were his only ticket. The wood stove was ready for winter, but he still needed to pile birch.

An old shipping container staged near the bottom of the trail where he parked let him lock his truck out of sight. He had only had the vehicle out twice during the summer and once earlier in the fall.

One thing Phil noticed was how much better his food tasted after working to get it himself. He never killed more than he needed, and until winter provided an outside freezer, he wasn't able to keep meat long unless he smoked it or preserved it. He fried the rabbit chunks in a sauce and ate it with a baked potato. The second rabbit was cut up and put into a simmering stew for the next day.

With food put aside, Phil cleaned up his shelter, starting in the kitchen area and working his way carefully around the entire place. Then he laid a cloth out on the small table. Unrolling his cleaning kit, he meticulously went over his gun, taking it apart and putting it back together. He kept his attention riveted on the process, taking his time with each step.

He had to invest himself completely into each task and give it one hundred percent of his time. He knew if he stopped living in the present he would be consumed by the past. As long as he was in the wild he was forced to focus on the present and the challenges it created.

Evenings had become a special time. His nightly duties and cleaning done, he would sit on the top of the cliff watching the open siding area to his left, along the tracks that ran below, or out across the lake spreading as far as the eye could see.

The clouds had moved on, replaced with a three-quarter moon. The wind was still present and he could see the moonlight shining off the whitecaps out on the water. Phil sat on a bench where he could hear the crashing waves over the wind as the sound swirled up against the rock.

He twisted the top off the stubby bottle, raising it towards the moon, the light shone through the clear amber liquid as the Crown Royal swished around in the bottle.

"Cheers to ya," he said to nobody.

The first hit of the bottle slammed into the back of his throat in a rush. The second one he swirled around in his mouth a moment, until he raised his head slightly and let it wash down. The bite of the liquor was good, even if his eyes squinted, his teeth clenched tight and his lips pressed together.

He rubbed away a dribble of whisky with the back of his arm and focused down below. Another big moose was wandering down the cleared siding. Phil had never seen so much wildlife. It was a nightly show.

He watched the animal as it made its way slowly along the track stopping to eat frequently. He liked that the animal was independent. The big moose wasn't worried about anything. He might run into trouble, but until then he was going about his own business without fear.

"Where you going?" he asked the moose as he tipped the bottle.

He couldn't stop his mind slipping backwards and grimaced. He'd had it pretty good in the city. Fuck, he'd had it all. The next drink was a longer one, burning as he took a slug.

"Don't go there," he said to himself.

The big moose turned off and headed through the thin line of trees towards the lake. Phil reached in to an inner pocket and pulled out a small carrying case. The Montecristo number fours and the whiskey were the only things he brought with him from the city and the small box of cigars back in his shelter was getting low, there were two or three left at the most.

Sniffing the cigar from one end to the other, he dug deep in his pocket and came out with clippers. A two-finger slice, and the rounded end was cut cleanly. Placing the cigar in his mouth, he clamped down gently with his teeth. The lighter flickered in the darkness and shadows jumped in his hands as he cupped them to keep out the wind.

Pulling the hood of his jacket up over his head, covering his ears, he took another hit of the Crown Royal. One hand rolled the cigar around lazily in his lips while he pondered the next day. He ought to get up early and get some fishing in on the Steel River.

The isolation and remoteness of the north shore kept the numbers of visitors down and the lakes were well stocked with pickerel, lake trout, and pike. But most of the rivers had been dammed for hydro, and were blocked at some point or another.

The Steel was undammed, one of the few flowing freely from a lake up on the northern shield down to Lake Superior. It was a three-hour walk for Phil, but was worth it at this time of year.

Sudden movement in his peripheral vision stopped him. He puffed on the cigar while staring down at the beach and let the movement organise itself into shapes.

"Well now, looks like company."

With the wind blowing away from him, the wolf had no notice as he came down the shoreline right into the moose's path. The wolf wasn't going to pass up any opportunity and quickly closed in on the bigger animal. He started to circle, attempting to get behind the moose. The big beast wasn't having any of it, matching the predator's moves as he circled in place keeping his rack towards the wolf.

The wolf charged in a few times from the front and had to be quick to duck out of the way, avoiding the deadly swings of the rack. When he did manage to get near the back of the moose he was met with battering ram kicks from the hind legs.

Phil thought about the nightlife and entertainment available in the city. The lights, noise, and things that money could buy. It couldn't touch this. This was real, nature at its wildest and he was there, part of it. He watched the two animals duel for half a cigar and then the wolf gave up. He must have decided he wasn't going to get anywhere, and had enough close calls to realize it wasn't worth it.

The wolf simply walked away, continuing on in the same direction he'd originally been heading, down towards the end of the beach and the rock cut below Phil. He wondered if such stalemates happened out here all the time.

Was he at a stalemate in life? And if he was, did it matter? Was he okay with it? He was sure that this way of living was sitting well with him, but he also knew that something just wasn't quite right.

"What's next?"

CHAPTER 5

Vancouver, 2012

The freighter sat anchored outside Vancouver harbor. Dragon was frustrated with the three-day wait for customs to get to the ship, but the delay had been taken into consideration and worked in his favor. They would dock today, ten days after their departure. They'd left on the eighth and arriving on the eighteenth was incredible luck.

Of course Dragon knew that you could influence luck and had worked hard to find this freighter with its auspicious schedule. He and Li wouldn't be getting off at the main shipping terminal, but would wait for the ship to unload and move to a different set of docks for scheduled maintenance. That was where they would sneak into Canada.

The TC associates in Vancouver would be at the maintenance facilities ready to shuttle them out once they landed. Li had two bags, just like Dragon. One of them filled with clothes and one with his machete. Dragon only brought along clothes and the M99. They had taken a long slow route on a freighter to ensure their ease of entry and the ability to bring their own equipment.

He'd forwarded his request for initial assistance in Vancouver through proper channels, and the local TC associates had assured them a competent soldier would be available to help with whatever he needed. The man had been respectful to Dragon from the start

"My name is Liang, it is an honor to assist you in any way."

Dragon thought about the name, Li stood for power and strength, Liang stood for bright and brilliant. Time will tell, he thought to himself.

"Good, I am Dragon and my friend is Li."

Dragon was unsure of the lay of the land in this city and didn't want to be a presence in local hotels, so he asked to be taken to a safe house. He was relieved to see the house provided was empty and he was able to relax as he sat in the living room. Liang sat opposite Dragon on a chair as Li checked the place out and cleared all the rooms.

"So, I wish to ask some questions."

"I will answer as best I can."

"I need to secure some labor, workers that I can control."

"We control most of the Chinese here in Vancouver. We can take whoever we want."

This was impressive. Dragon knew there were millions of Chinese in this city alone and still more across Canada. Obviously the triads had a good footing.

"How is this done?"

"Immigrants are encouraged to settle in specific areas, those who decide to settle in other sections are identified and targeted until they comply. Once grouped together the process is the same as anywhere else. Divide and control."

Dragon was starting to like this soldier. The man had more insight than he'd expected. He had more questions about the Chinese in Vancouver and the triad control, but got back to his mission.

"Okay, tomorrow we get some workers. What about soldiers? I need four or five men who can be counted on completely."

"I will talk with my boss and have an answer for you quickly."

*****

The plan was to get a team together and drive across Canada by car. There would be no paper trails. Dragon wanted all the pieces to fall into place, workers, soldiers and transportation. No one would have any idea what was up. Just that they were on a mission.

Liang and another soldier showed up the next day around noon with a van, they opened the vehicle's side doors and escorted four men into the house. Dragon knew these were the workers, because they sure weren't soldiers.

Liang lined the men up in front of him. "These men are eager to help in any way they can."

"How can you assure me that they won't run if they get the chance?"

"We know where their families are and we are watching them. We will be watching them until these men complete their work."

"Good." Dragon was again impressed with the triad's control. He knew in the back of his head that if his great-grandfather's riddle ended in failure he would be able to expand the family business from Vancouver.

"Show them to a room where they can wait."

Liang moved the men to the basement and returned to Dragon.

"You were quick to get me men Liang, how about the soldiers?"

"My boss has told me be at your assistance for as long as you need me. He said to get the men myself and to be available."

"Make sure these men are your toughest and most loyal. Have them ready to leave tomorrow."

"I'll do this."

"We will need two vehicles for the morning as well. Is that a problem?"

"No. Everything will be ready."

*****

Dragon loved the Rocky Mountains. After the two-car convoy left Vancouver heading east, they'd hit Kamloops, Salmon Arm and Revelstoke. He was reminded of his connection to the mountains back home.

He knew if he came back to Vancouver to start a business he'd be settling in these parts, but that didn't matter at this point. The only thing that mattered right now was the ghost town of Jackfish. The more he thought about the story, the more it intrigued him.

The place was completely abandoned. The whole north shore of Ontario's Lake Superior was remote and isolated. How did a Scandinavian fishing village end up there in the first place? The answer in that neck of the woods was the railroad. Once a rail siding was installed it needed to be manned and a telegraph station put in. Right on the lakeshore, a fishing village would now have a way to ship their fish immediately by train to Toronto and Montreal.

The town could have remained like that, but then it was made a coal-reloading stop for the trains and a major dock was put in. It dwarfed the fishermen's small docks, acting like a break wall for them.

With the additional workers arriving to unload the coal and service the trains, there was soon a small collection of houses. When the schoolhouse was built the town was in full swing.

Dragon knew his great-grandfather had been there well before the town began. He was beginning to appreciate the journey that the man must have been on. The land would have been untamed and inaccessible, yet they had built a railroad by hand from one end of the country to the other through rock and mountain.

When Canadian Pacific changed to diesel locomotives they needed more land for multiple sidings and closed up Jackfish, moving to a larger, flatter area further down the line. When the workers left to follow the company the writing was on the wall for the town. A big fire at the old hotel finished the job.

A ghost town. It didn't matter how many times he thought about it, he was still curious as hell. What did you find Tiger? What were those *steel eyes*?

When their convoy hit the prairies both Li and Dragon were astounded by the landscape. Flat for hours upon hours. Now the size of the country was becoming real. Two of Liang's soldiers traded off driving duties in the second car carrying the four workers.

Another soldier drove the first car with Liang beside him. Dragon and Li were in the back seat. The trip had been going as planned until a big truck got between the two vehicles. Their driver wanted to slow and let the truck pass so the second car could catch up. The truck driver wasn't having any of it, driving his eighteen-wheeler right up to their back window.

The soldier swerved a bit as the trucker got close, then tried to accelerate. The trucker just sped up, staying on the car's tail. The soldier slowed again, hoping the accelerating truck would pull out and pass.

A blaring horn was the only response as the truck's engine roared just inches from their bumper. The soldier accelerated again suddenly pulling off the road, slamming on the brakes. The car slid sideways on the gravel shoulder, almost into the ditch, before the driver managed to swing it back onto the shoulder and slow to a stop.

The big truck flew by, his horn still blaring in a solid complaint. Everyone was swearing and shaking their heads in the car except Li, he was memorizing the colors of the truck. Finally the cars regrouped and continued into Winnipeg.

Stopping for a meal at a roadside truck stop near the Ontario border, Li disappeared briefly. Once the car was moving again Dragon watched the smile spreading across Li's face.

"Out with it Li, what's so amusing?"

"I took care of that truck driver at the rest stop. That one who had been following us and giving us trouble back there on the road."

Dragon was shocked, Liang was turned around in his seat staring at Li as well. The incident had happened six hours earlier. Dragon spoke first, "How could you possible know it was the right man?"

"I got a good look at the colors of the truck. It was the right truck." He seemed satisfied with himself.

"What colors and what truck?" Liang didn't like things happening he didn't know about.

"It was red and green and had the driver's name on the truck, Dillon Transport."

"Jesus Christ, Li! There are hundreds of those trucks. Look there!" Liang pointed to another of the red and green Dillon Transports that was flying down the highway in the opposite direction. "Is that the one?"

Li watched the truck sail by and realized he wasn't so sure now. He turned to Dragon and shrugged his shoulders. Dragon laughed out loud. "Li you need to take it easy, let our escort, young Liang, take care of the issues for now."

Liang sat in the front seat shaking his head.

*****

Dick Reimer was heading west to Victoria, BC. Starting out at five that morning, he stopped for the night at the Husky truck stop west of Kenora. He liked the Husky's hot meals and showers. After cleaning up and eating he had a few beer. The third one was a little much after a long day and he was feeling a nice glow.

He planned another early morning tomorrow so paid up his bill and headed out to crawl in the sleeper. He flirted with the idea of calling a hooker, this was close enough to a major centre to find one easily, but it was early in the trip and he had some women along the route he could visit for free.

Unlocking the door, he leaned back to open it and started to climb up into the cab. The hard push from behind was so sudden that Dick couldn't react. He went over sideways, falling over the seat, narrowly avoiding smacking his head on the floor.

What the fuck? As he tried to right himself he noticed a man in the doorway at the same time as a fist smashed into the side of his face. He went over again, this time crumpling onto the floor between the seats. He tried to shake himself awake as he felt his attacker step over him, grabbing his coat collar and dragging him into the sleeper.

Dick got his head on straight in a hurry, this was serious. He took a breath and tried to fight back. He kicked out with his leg and caught the fucker, felt him go backwards. Here was his chance. He turned on his knees, trying to get up.

A crazy Chinese lunged at him and struck him in the chest and head. Dick's neck snapped back against the sleeper's bed and he tried to punch upwards at the attacker's head above. The guy slid down his chest and straddled Dick's legs. He had Dick by the hair and was staring him in the face, inches away.

Dick was horrified, the look on the man's face was sadistic, then he spoke. "You fuck around with us?"

He couldn't understand the language, it sounded Chinese or something. "I don't know what you mean. Who are you?"

The man's other hand came up beside Dick's head and in a quick motion plunged a short knife into the side of his neck. Dick felt the blade in his throat and liquid filling his mouth. He wanted to scream, but choked instead.

He tried to focus on the Chinese man. He couldn't believe what was happening, he wanted to ask why.

"You don't mess with us again."

Again the strange language. Dick still didn't understand what the man meant, but it didn't matter, he had to swallow. The blood was pouring out of his mouth and neck. The sudden jerk as the knife was pulled out shocked him. Then there was a whistling noise. Then there was nothing.

CHAPTER 6

Jackfish, 1883

Things picked up for the Chinese when they got to the landing that would become Jackfish siding. They were no longer pushing forward. The crews worked for a week to clear an opening up and level it for the two sets of tracks.

The workers, who usually slept in tents and were constantly on the move, were able to quickly construct wooden shelters over their tents that were mainly four posts with a log roof. Tiger used his influence with the bosses to allow the structures and then demanded higher payments from the workers for the comfort.

There were a few workers who tried to buck the system and were talking of refusing to pay him. These men disappeared and any others who had been listening to their talk soon forgot what they had heard.

The white bosses used Tiger more and more. He seemed to get better results from the Chinese workers than they could themselves and the railway was making good time even in these harsh conditions.

It was clear that they were going to start pushing forward again in the next day or two and they'd be back to constantly moving their tents. To Tiger it didn't matter, stopped or moving he was making money and his only concern was that the cash was piling up. With nowhere to put the money it was bulging out of the sack he stored it in, becoming harder to carry around.

On Thursday everyone was in the camp taking the day off. The torrent of rain that pounded down on them over night and into the day was washing away line and causing flash flooding off the hills. The men huddled in their tents sleeping, drinking or gambling.

Tiger and Bao were strategizing in their own tent. "The money is becoming hard to handle Bao. There's too much of it."

"And everyone knows we have it."

"We have got to get away from the track, or find something to do with the money."

The men were silent as they worked through the problem.

"I think the money is too good to leave," Bao volunteered. "We should collect it as long as we can."

Tiger agreed, but they still had to deal with the cash they were already carrying.

"Okay, let's hide the money here, we'll always be able to find this siding."

The two men bagged up the bills in multiple leather layers and ensured the package was watertight. They would use the cover of the pouring rain to slip out of camp and find a hiding spot.

Walking east, past the end of the rails that had been laid the day before, they kept going. Tiger was doing his best to pick out their surroundings in the heavy rain. The stakes planted ahead showed the projected track leading away from the camp.

He examined the two large hills framing the area, they would always be recognisable. Tiger wanted to turn off into the woods, but needed a spot he would be sure to remember.

Continuing to watch, he looked for the perfect spot as they pushed forward in the rain. Finally he stopped and looked at Bao. "We'll turn here."

Bao nodded and the two men angled off through the knee-high brush. As they began encountering thicker brush and bigger trees Tiger pushed on through the branches, getting scratched for his trouble.

He wanted to bury the bags. The forest was too thick where they were, so he continued to push onward. Suddenly he popped through the tree line into a small clearing. The forest surrounded them on all sides of the opening, backing up against the jagged side of the hill.

"This is the spot Bao, only the two of us will know. We'll come back later and get it."

Bao nodded and the two of them began to dig a hole big enough for the three bags. Taking turns they kept making the hole deeper. It wasn't the first time they'd buried money and Tiger thought about the mountains in China.

He looked up at the hill. The moss that grew on the rocks fascinated him and while he let Bao dig he peeled some of the soft green stuff off the rock. There was a seam of color that was different, white against the gray of the granite. The seam widened as it got to ground level and he peeled back more of the moss.

What?

Tiger felt his head get a little light and begin to float. He reached out one hand and steadied himself against the rock wall.

Was it possible?

He looked down at Bao who was still digging and tried to think. His head swirled. What was he going to do with this? He stepped away from the rock wall and eased around behind Bao. He knew he had choices, but they all came to the same conclusion.

This was too big a secret to share.

He felt the pain that was coming before he did a thing. It hurt him to do this, but it was the only way he could guarantee this secret stayed with the family. He stepped close to Bao's back and pulled out the long-bladed knife he kept attached at his waist.

There was no use thinking. It would only make it worse. His shoulder muscles tensed as Tiger brought the knife up. Reaching forward, he wrapped an arm around his long-time friend and pulled back hard. Drawing a red line across Bao's neck only took a second. Bao didn't even react.

*****

He had been shocked at first, then stunned when he felt the knife cutting into his throat. His head angled up and he saw Tiger's hand pointing to something. Bao wanted to understand but he couldn't.

Why was Tiger killing him? They were like brothers. Then his eye caught something and his heart started to pound with excitement. He felt Tiger turning him over and the two men locked eyes. Bao could see the tears running down Tiger's face and knew that what he had done hadn't been easy.

"Forgive me my friend. Do you see it is bigger than us? Do you understand?" There was horror in Tiger's face along with regret and anger. "Please Bao, forgive me."

The last moments of Bao's life were spent reaching forward to grab hold and pull his friend forward. Tiger lowered his head to hear Bao's last words.

"I will miss you, take care of your wealth."

*****

Tiger sat in the rain holding his friend and cried until the tears wouldn't come any more. Why did his future have to lead to this? Someday he would understand that he'd done the right thing, but right now he felt alone in the world and his new discovery brought him little relief.

He finished burying the money alongside his friend. Dragging up some dead wood he leaned it up against the hill, covering what he had found. He knew it would hurt again when he came back, but his friend deserved to be remembered, the memories respected. When he was done hiding his find it was hard to leave.

Without Bao he knew things wouldn't be the same. The rain felt colder on his shoulders as he walked back to the camp.

*****

The work crews were going to be hard at it again starting the next morning. The pounding rain had stopped. Tiger had been trying to deal with himself ever since the afternoon. Sitting alone in his tent he was racked with guilt and full of excitement at the same time. The far off sound of a locomotive inching up the newly built rail pulled him from his thoughts.

When he went outside to meet the engine, he was joined by all the other Chinese who were just as curious as he was. This train was bringing supplies to continue the track. They'd see it every month or so. It was still a distraction for everyone.

Tiger was always interested in new supplies because he would have to decide what part of the shipment he would secure for his workers. This resulted in him being able to increase the amount he would, in turn, charge each of them weekly. Just when Tiger thought his day was already upside down, he watched it go from bad to worse.

The train stopped and men started unloading. The first man off the crew car at the back was an immediate threat. This one was clearly a gangster and wasn't afraid to show it. He'd stepped off first to ensure that everyone saw him.

The next twenty men climbing down from the train sporting tattoos gave Tiger an uneasy feeling in the pit of his stomach. Then he thought of Bao. *What have I done?*

Later that evening he had a visitor. The man announced himself outside Tiger's tent. "May I come in?"

Tiger knew that sooner or later it had to happen. "Yes, join me." He also knew who it would be.

The man who had been first off the train opened up the tent flap, ducking inside. He stood up tall and squared his feet. Now he was staring down at Tiger.

"Welcome to the railroad," he smiled at the newcomer. "Welcome to hell."

The guy was clearly dangerous. His cocky attitude and the numerous scars on his arms and face said he wasn't scared of getting dirty.

"My name is Meng. How many workers are there here?"

This one was getting right to the point. There would be no casual conversation. He knew there wouldn't be a good ending to this discussion either. Now it was all about maintaining face and he knew his moment was coming. So he answered, "Close to five hundred. More now with the new ones."

"You take protection money from these people?" The gangster's menacing look transferred itself into the question.

"This would be your concern in what way?" Tiger wasn't planning to back down from anyone. He did register the scowl of annoyance on the gangster's face at his answer.

The gangster revealed a 14K symbol on the inner part of his forearm. Tiger shifted his shirt and revealed the symbol he had above his TC tattoo. He noted the surprise on the gangster's face. The tough guy hadn't expected that. Tiger was higher up the food chain.

He knew it wouldn't matter once the gangster thought it through. They were out here in the middle of nowhere and forcing other people out was okay if you could get away with it. This far from China no one would even know. Tiger hoped his tactic bought him some time to think while the criminal figured out his next move.

"Me and my men plan to become involved with the countrymen. I hope we don't have problems between us." The threat was clear.

"You should hope not." Tiger stayed tough.

Meng stood and nodded. "These wood shelters are nice."

"My crews are leaving in the morning, so they'll be empty soon."

Meng wasn't listening. He was bent over and moving out of the tent.

*****

Tiger met with the rail bosses in the morning as they geared up to start laying line again. He had become respected for the amount of progress he could generate. When he was asked whether he wanted more men for his crew from the new arrivals he jumped at the opening he'd been hoping for.

"You will need to watch these men Mr. Boss. The new ones with the tattoos are trouble. If they get mixed up with the front crew it will slow us down for sure." He explained that they would force the others to slow down to an easy pace, that threats and violence were all they knew. "They would be better used at the rear in some other labor positions."

"Okay Tiger, we'll keep your crew as it is. Go clear me some line."

"Yes, Mr. Boss."

That was one problem taken care of. Experience said that the newcomers would be rested a day and put to work the next. Tiger hoped his crew was well ahead by then and could stay that way.

He had to get off this railroad as soon as possible. He might, or might not win the battle, but make no mistake, there was one coming. He might be able to rally the others and hope the numbers would be enough. Five hundred to twenty sounded like good odds.

Unfortunately, he knew that explicit threats and outright violence could also convert some of the men to the other side. He should have left by now, but after his incredible find the other day he knew he had to get out as soon as possible. He realized before he did anything else he had better write down news of his discovery and make sure it got back to China. Even if he didn't.

CHAPTER 7

Jackfish, 2012

Phil stepped down to the edge of the river. Every time he came here it was exciting. He knew he was almost guaranteed a fish on the first cast, which was friggin' amazing. He'd done some fishing down south, ending up standing shoulder to shoulder in a crowd of other fishermen lining the banks while the fish were running up the rivers to spawn.

Down there it always seemed like the fish were finicky and you had to get everything just right, from line length, weights, to the size and color of bait. Even then the fish could just nibble evasively. What a hell of a difference it was up north.

Phil wasn't even what he'd call an avid fisherman, but he found fish heaven on the Steel. Most rivers get smaller the farther you go upriver until they are too narrow and shallow for fish. A normal spawning season would see the fish spawn and head back down the river, usually dying on the way back to the lake.

The Steel River had a lake on either end, so the fish ran from Superior up to the smaller lake along a river that had nice channels the entire way. The remoteness and lack of hydro dams made it pristine. Phil knew that typically it was rainbow trout in the spring and salmon, brown specks, and rainbow again in the fall.

The rainbow would run all fall, mixing in with the different salmon runs that came one after another. First pink salmon, then Coho followed by Chinook. He loved the rainbow.

"Okay, let's have some fun."

He wanted to cast his lure in just the right spot. He aimed just below the big spruce tree clinging to the bank overhanging his target. The channel was deep near the other bank with trees marking the top and bottom of the drift. He knew his best chance for the big one was on his first cast.

If a smaller fish took the lure as he reeled it in, the commotion caused by fighting it to the shore would usually spook the big one and it would probably be lost for the day. Phil reached his arm back and then his rod flew forward as he cast the lure out, aiming below the tree.

The lure hit with a slash, just above the drift. He reeled in a bit as the current swept the line over the deep channel. He let the lure float down as far as it could before the next tree then started to reel it in, bringing it back up through the drift.

Bang!

The line went tight and the tip of the rod started to bend, at the same time a silver rainbow broke the top of the water. Phil watched as his line kept pulling under the water while the trout danced in the air. Flap, flap, and the fish splashed down on its side.

He reeled until he had tension on the line, rod held high up in the air. The fish headed downriver and Phil felt line spin out as he held his rod pointed upriver. He didn't want the thing to run for the lake, he needed it to stay in this hole. The fish jumped again, this time making a long arc, like a dolphin, before falling back into the water.

Rod up in the air, holding the fish there, he felt it turn and come back upriver. He reeled hard to keep up. He knew he had a nice one, at least seven or more pounds and obviously fresh from the lake. The fresh ones put up a lot more fight. Fish that had been hanging around the river awhile were beat up from the rocks and the struggles of the spawning run.

This one came out of the water with enough force that it lost its own balance and went head over fins in a flip before slapping the surface of the water. *Splash*. He realized he was laughing out loud.

"Go baby, go."

The battle went on for minutes. The beautiful sound of line zinging out as the fish ran in surges and the song of the reel as he cranked hard to get him back in. Finally the fish began to tire and he knew he had this one. He nursed it to shore, pulling it up on the gravel edge of the bank. The trout's shine was incredible, he could see the rainbow effect all along the side of the fish.

It was that easy. He couldn't believe it. He could get another fish out of the same drift right now. He wouldn't make it a mile up the river and he'd have ten fish out of the other holes if he wanted, but he was only here to take a couple.

Enjoying the scenery, he decided to leave this hole alone and walk up to the next sweet spot. That hole was on a corner with a set of rapids just above it. It was deeper that the first one and Phil took a breath, setting himself before casting, he was sure there was going to be another fish.

Standing at the top of the hole, close to the end of the rapids, he cast down to the bottom of the pool. Slowly he brought his lure back through the water towards the rapids. The current was putting nice pressure on the lure, ensuring he would feel it when a fish hit.

Bang!

"Hello."

Phil reefed the rod upwards to set the hook. Now he had to keep the line tight and wait to see what he had. He could tell this fish wasn't as big as the other as it flew left and right, from one side of the hole to the other, trying to escape. That was fine with him unless it started to go down river.

Fighting the thing back and forth, he didn't see the fish until the fight was almost done. Oh, he liked that, a brown speckled trout. It was at least three pounds, with some wild coloring. The top was dark, almost black, the sides were a brown and gold with orange spots and finally the bottom fins were black with white tips.

Once he had it off the lure he held the brookie up in the air, letting the sun reflect off it. It looked awesome. No doubt it was going for food. He looked up the river and knew he had to make a point of camping out here sometime and exploring farther up. The idea of cooking the fish right on the shore was appealing.

Today was done. It had taken three hours walking along the tracks from Jackfish to the river and he still had to make his way back, this time carrying the two fish. Luckily, he'd left at five this morning. Looking up at the sun he was sure it was only around noon.

Phil took the time to clean the fish on the edge of the water. Same thing as usual, he wanted to get rid of the waste before he headed back. The bald eagles that called this river home would make short work of the leftovers.

*****

Walking along the tracks on the way back to the shelter the past caught up to Phil again. He was thinking about sharing the fishing experience he'd had that day with someone. With his mind occupied it had been a perfect morning, now he was back fighting to forget and move on.

He welcomed the rock-cuts he had to walk through for the shade. He knew he had to watch for trains, you just didn't want to be stuck against a granite wall with a train flying by inches from your face. He thought it might suck you right off the wall into certain death under the metal wheels.

This rock-cut was the biggest around, much larger than the one he lived on, but it did mean he was getting close to home. He hurried his step a bit as he always did in the cuts. The growl scared the shit out of him. The loud sound echoed off the bare rock.

Phil dropped his rod and slung the fish chain down beside it. He had the rifle off his shoulder, pulling it around in front of his chest in a hurry. He stood there looking forward and back along the track. The next growl wasn't as loud, almost not as menacing. He was able to follow the source of the sound better and raised his head.

Still not seeing anything, he looked up the steep cliff examining the ledges and crevices running top to bottom. Then something moved.

"Jesus."

The cougar looked stuck about two thirds of the way up. *How the hell did he get there?* Was he pushed over the top by something? It was possible. But maybe he'd been scared by a train and tried to run up the face. Either way, he was on a slim ledge with nowhere to go.

Surveying the rock face, he confirmed that the cougar must have come down from the top, gotten onto the ledge and realized he couldn't go any further and had come too far to turn around. Then he wondered if the cat had been sitting there when he walked by in the morning. If it had, it had been keeping quiet.

"You asking for some help?"

Phil had to get out of the cut before a train came. He decided to go and see what the situation looked like from above. Leaving the rod at the end of the cut, he went around the side of the hill. He kept the fish tied to his belt and the rifle slung downward across his chest for the climb. He didn't need to come back down to missing fish. The climbs around here were brutal and he went hand-to-hand, from rock to tree, in a steady accent to the top.

Finally, he walked along the top, trying to find the spot where the cougar went down. He located a patch where it looked like the edge of the cliff had fallen away, and stared down at the animal. The cat was a lot closer from here. They watched each other, while the cougar let out a series of low growls.

How long had he been there? He might be real hungry, which bothered Phil. He took the brown trout off his waist and dropped it down to the big cat, hoping it didn't bounce off the ledge. The cougar looked at the fish and back at Phil. The cat ignored it for now.

Could he help the animal out? Not with the other fish around, he wanted that one for himself. He wasn't far from his place and with a last look at the cougar, he headed back down the side of the hill. It didn't take more than an hour to take the other fish home, drop off his fishing gear and get back to the cat.

He was carrying his rifle and machete when he arrived back at the top of the rock-cut. The old bush blade was ancient but it was heavy and it was sharp. Once he was looking down at the cougar again he knew there was only one thing to do, lower a thick branch or log down to the ledge and let him figure it out on his own. Hopefully that would give Phil some time to get out of there.

The adrenaline pumping through his veins wasn't a surprise. He always felt it when he was heading into something with serious consequences. His face flushed and his neck muscles tightened as the extra energy mixed with pictures of his past. He shook his head. He needed to focus on the here and now, and be in the present.

"Dammit Phil. Wake up."

Looking around for a good branch, he found a small dead tree laying on the ground fifteen feet away. That would do. He took the machete and cut it away from the stump but left the dead branches on it. Dragging it over to the cliff he looked down at the cougar. The fish was completely gone, bones and all.

"Thought so," he smiled. "All right cat, get out of the way."

Trying to turn the tree and drop it onto a thin ledge was hard enough without the additional worry of hitting the cougar. He'd let the cat figure that out on his own as well. The bottom of the tree slipped over the edge while Phil held the branches at the top as tight as he could, no sense in losing it now.

He half guided it onto the ledge and found a rock to wedge it against. At the top he found a crack in the granite hillside and tried to wedge one of the branches in there to hold it. Phil stood back three or four steps and looked down at the cougar. He decided he better get his ass out of there.

The cougar had been pushed to the narrow end of the ledge to avoid the tree, but as soon as Phil stepped away the cat surged upward. The cat scraped and clawed his way up the tree to the top of the cliff.

Shit! Now what? Phil took a few more steps backwards holding the rifle. He noticed his hands weren't as steady as usual.

The cougar reached the top in a rush and jumped from the tree to the ground, landing softly. The big cat turned towards him, and they locked eyes. Phil was glad the gun was in his hands, he knew he couldn't move if he tried. It would take everything he had to pull the trigger if required.

The cougar let out a slow growl that tailed off at the end, broke his stare, turned and walked into the bush, leaving Phil standing there.

Outstanding, was all he could think.

Until he realized he should be gone.

High-tailing it out of there, he was back in the safety of his shelter within the hour.

*****

From the hilltop the moon was bright enough to see the shadows cast by the trees. Phil looked down at what he was starting to call his television; the open area along the rail siding. Tonight he could see the whole area and led his eyes past it and down the tracks for a mile or so.

The fish and rice cooked over the open fire had been excellent. He'd cleaned up meticulously and sat to break down his rifle again. It was more an exercise than a need, he hadn't fired it since doing some targeting to zero in the sights when he first arrived.

He pulled out the half-cigar left over from the other night and lit it up. He looked down at the bottle and hesitated a moment before spinning the top off and tipping it up for a taste. Sucking in some air, he waited to feel the warmth of the liquid going down.

"Now that was nice." An involuntary shake spread the warmth through his body and made him tip the bottle up again.

Time slipped by as he talked to the wind and fought to control his rising anger. His face showed stress, then concern, before he finally settled with his teeth clenched and a scowl on his face. He belonged in the wild, he needed to get used to it and bring himself around to it. He sure wasn't going back.

Phil froze. Something was moving in the trees to his left. He heard it again, a branch snapping. He reached slowly for the rifle, bringing it up on his lap. Time seemed suspended as he waited for the next sound. He didn't turn to look. He wanted to react to what ever happened instead of relying on his eyesight in the dark.

The growl wasn't angry, just carried lightly across to Phil as he fought not to turn. He wasn't pissed at the cougar for coming to his shelter, he knew the cat lived somewhere nearby, but he was still concerned that it was willing to come so close to a human.

"Hey, big fella."

He waited an hour before finally moving his head and then turning his body. He stood up and looked around. He hadn't heard a thing since the slight growl. Was he just being checked out? Had he been followed home?

One thing was sure, if he was going to live up here, he would be seeing more of the cat.

CHAPTER 8

2012 Terrace Bay

April Harrison was pretty much the law in these parts. The thirty-four year old had been an Ontario Provincial Police officer for ten years, working out of the Schreiber OPP station. She covered Schreiber and Terrace Bay, two remote towns on the top of Lake Superior. For the next few weeks she was on day shift while the other officer had nights.

April grew up in the area and knew it like the back of her hand. She'd turned down opportunities to move up in the ranks, primarily because she wanted to stay where she was. Promotions meant new assignments at new locations.

It was an easy job up here and it had become routine. Aside from a few accidents on the TransCanada highway and the odd drunk to get home, or stick in a cell for the night. She did her rounds in the big black and white four-by-four, giving out the odd ticket. Well, enough to meet her quota anyway.

Today she was running radar. Partially concealed in a snowplow turn-around, she sat with the front end of the cruiser pointed up the highway. There wasn't much that happened in her area that she wasn't on top of. She believed in being proactive, and usually knew who was a problem and where the trouble would start. Generally she could keep ahead of it.

April only had one real problem, well, actually two. She didn't have a man in her life right now. That was probably the only downfall she could see in staying up north. There wasn't a shortage of interested parties, but setting aside the married ones and the mavericks that just wanted a side of fun, she wasn't getting any.

Her second problem was her biggest mistake. Brad Harrison had seemed like the perfect guy when she had returned from training in the south and took up her current position. Settle down, think about kids, the white picket fence, blah, blah. God, what a frikkin' disaster.

She didn't want to think about it. Rehashing the old memories just put her in a bad mood, which was bad timing for the SUV heading her way, ten kilometres over the speed limit. She'd recently given up smoking and that was enough aggravation to tip the scale in favour of writing this guy a ticket. She raised her hand and snapped on the cherries.

The speeding SUV would see her lights as the cruiser moved out of its hiding place. She just assumed everyone would pull over. There was always a chance she'd get a runner. She'd had a few in the last ten years and was never really ready for them. This guy did as she expected and she listened to his whining with half an ear as she gave him the ticket.

The afternoon was getting on, and she wanted to get in a late lunch. She knew exactly where to go. The little bar was tucked away in the back of Schreiber. The only occupants would be Canadian Pacific rail workers and retirees. The old timers from the maintenance yard gathered daily to reminisce and have a few drinks. The food was good and the workers came in regularly throughout the day, which meant that the cook was always manning the stove.

This was one of her pulse points, where she got a feel for the crews and their mood going into the weekend. It wouldn't be the first time she watched someone being rowdy and throwing a few back, then later she'd be called out to deal with the same guy as the drinking went on into the night.

Thursday the place was nearly empty. The only customers, four old-timers, were well into their afternoon beer. April ordered a sandwich and salad and sat down in a booth at the back of the century-old converted train station. She scanned the large screen TV hanging over the bar, but it was tuned to some dumb sports channel.

"Who's the guy livin' down at Jackfish?"

April's daydream broke. The old guys were staring and she realized they were taking to her. "Pardon me guys, what was that?"

"Who's that guy livin' down at Jackfish?"

This wasn't the first time she'd heard that someone might be living down there. She reminded herself that she had to make a point of confirming that one way or the other. She had the odd house out that way she watched over, but none at Jackfish. If someone was down there she'd have to check in every once in a while. Besides, what was the guy doing there?

"I didn't know there was someone down there," she raised her eyebrows. "What have you guys been hearing?"

"Thought you knew everything." The old-timer laughed and took a swig of his beer. He liked to pull anyone's leg, and hers would do fine.

"Seriously, what have you heard?" April wasn't biting.

The table was silent for a minute then one of them offered, "The boys are saying that he's like a wild man. Has hair all over and a big bushy beard. The train crews say he's been there for months, always walking around carrying a rifle."

"How do they know he's living there?"

"When they come through at night they see a fire burning or lights up on the hill above the old ghost town."

"I might have to get down and have a look. Thanks."

The joker was quick to pounce. "Ya ought to do somethin', besides hanging out in a bar all day."

"No, we can't all do that, now can we?" The joker's friends laughed at his expense.

April was back on the road heading out of town. She'd planned on setting up another radar trap to kill a few hours and just relax in the fall sun. Now this guy at Jackfish was on her mind.

She didn't care who lived there, as long as she was on top of it. This curiosity had worked well for her so far and she wouldn't ignore it now. She turned around in another roadside pull-out used by the snowplows and targeted her radar up the road again. She wanted a few more tickets, they were calling for rain over the next few days and she wouldn't want to be getting wet if she didn't have to.

*****

April's shift was over and she'd given in to her inner prompting. Instead of heading back to the station, she headed east from Terrace Bay on the twenty-minute drive to Jackfish. She was going to check this thing out and see what was going on.

The only reason the long gravel road down the hill was kept open was for the railroad siding. Even though the railway had long ago gone to electrical switching of the rails, the crews still needed to get down there and maintain the switch boxes.

She'd never thought much about the place, but as she drove down she was reminded that there had been a town here at one time. Suddenly she realized she didn't have all the answers like usual. A stranger in a ghost town. *Great, what next?*

April slowed down as she neared the open area around the siding to scan ahead and watch for anything out of the ordinary. She looked up at the top of the hills that framed the old station and its town.

It would take a serious climb to the top. And that wasn't getting done today, which was a disappointment. The next best thing was looking around the bottom. She drove along the tracks on the gravel service road, towards the hill at the end of the siding. The old road into the town had originally wound its way around the back of the hills and she assumed there was still an old half-washed out goat path that struggled up and around to the other side.

April couldn't follow the road far and wouldn't try. She wouldn't want to get stuck this far out of Terrace Bay, there were spots in the granite hills where the radios didn't work, and she didn't want to have to walk a couple miles back up to the highway.

She was about to drive away from the small road when something caught her attention. The sun was now behind the hill, but visibility was still clear enough that she picked up the shape. That's what stood out. It was too square for the forest.

Parking the truck, she got out to investigate. Walking up the old road twenty paces, she realized what it was. The dark brown storage container was one of the full size ones used to transport cargo on the freight trains. *What the hell?*

What was it doing here and why? She walked around it and noticed the door was secured with a chain and padlock, so someone was using it. Looking down, she couldn't make out any recent tracks. It could belong to the railroad. Maybe storage for tools. The thing was backed up into the forest, just off the old trail. It almost looked like it had been deliberately camouflaged with long branches laid against it and brush piled on top.

The railroad crews wouldn't hide their stuff like that.

She checked the old road a little further along and didn't see any real evidence of tracks there either. It looked like she would have to walk around the hills, or climb to the top. Neither option was attractive right now. As April thought more about it, she realized she was going to have to come earlier in the day to give herself more time, or she would have to come at night and try to see the lights that were supposed to be on top of the hill.

Returning to her truck, she slowly drove back out along the siding. She stopped and got out at the far end of the clearing, just before the road turned back up towards the highway and stared for a moment at the hills rising up at the other end of the clearing.

Running her eyes over the top of the hill there was only rock and tree. She was turning her head for a second look when her eyes picked up a brief flash of light. She stopped and focused, but saw nothing more.

Interesting. She was sure she'd seen something abnormal. Something reflecting the last rays of sun, either glass or steel, but just that once. Well, now she had both a personal curiosity and a professional interest.

April smiled to herself, was he up there now? She put the truck into gear and headed back up towards the TransCanada.

*****

Phil liked knowing that he could hear vehicles as they came down the gravel road. Usually it was the CP crews going to the switching box or to work on equipment they left at the siding overnight. Sometimes a train would pull in off the track with rail equipment and wait for someone from the main base in Schreiber to come and get them.

Over the summer there had been travelers looking for a place to park off the TransCanada for the night, or day trippers down to explore along the shore line. They usually never stayed long. The noise of the passing trains usually chased away the campers after the first night.

"Well, well, well. What have we here?"

The black and white of the OPP cruiser was like a flashback. He felt a number of confusing feelings. Concern and interest, even anger and fear.

"Damn."

He moved to the edge of the hill to get a better look. The cop's truck was slowly moving down beside the track towards the rock-cut. At his end of the siding it turned away from the rails and headed along the base of the hill. Phil wondered if it was a coincidental drive-through or if the cop was there with a purpose in mind.

He heard the truck shut off but couldn't see down at that steep an angle from where he was. The cop had to be close to the container, which wasn't much of a concern. He hardly used it and hadn't been there in a few months. He wondered what was happening down below. He could fee a little sweat on his palms as he held the gun.

There was relief when the truck started up again and he watched it crawl along the siding until it was back across the clearing. Phil raised the rifle and looked through the scope to watch the truck leave, keeping it trained on the vehicle as it came to a stop.

When the woman got out and started looking around Phil took a second to check her out. Confident by the way she stood, and athletic. He reached up to adjust the scope and noticed she looked up towards the hill at the same time. Then he saw her stop and stare right at him.

"Double damn."

Phil lowered the rifle tip to the ground and stared with his own eyes. She was a smart one, that was sure, she might have seen him somehow, the scope probably, he wondered what that meant.

He needed a drink.

CHAPTER 9

Dragon had been planning as they drove, picking up things they might need, including food and supplies for the workers. He needed a little bit of everything because he had no idea what he was looking for.

His anticipation was being replaced with excitement as they neared the Jackfish turn-off. He'd traded in one vehicle for a pick-up truck and trailer that looked like a million other travellers on the road. The triad owned rental agency made sure there would be no paper trail. The soldiers were set up in the closest motel, just ten kilometres back along the highway. He had acquired some good sat phones which they would use for communication.

Now just him, the workers, and Li drove down the gravel road, following the directions the motel owner told them was the only way into Jackfish. Dragon drove at a crawl to prevent the sound of their arrival from travelling in the quiet darkness. He had no idea what to expect.

When they reached the opening in the forest he could see the two separate rail lines, which meant they were at the siding, he ordered a stop. "Li you take care of the men, I need to take a walk."

Dragon went over to the track and looked both ways. The rails came from the east and split in two here at the siding. He followed along them towards the other end of the clearing. Looking back at the trailer he knew he was far enough out of sight.

Reaching into his inner pocket he pulled out a piece of paper wrapped in plastic. He couldn't read it in the dark, but knew the words by heart. He just wanted to feel the paper in his hands.

"Okay Tiger, speak to me."

The words all described things he needed to see, which was useless this late at night, but he was filled with nervous energy and could at least orient himself. He followed the siding until it joined back up with the main line at the west end of the clearing.

Here where the rail lines joined together before entering the rock-cut, Dragon realized he'd found his first hill. He continued to walk along the tracks. Thirty paces into the cut and the walls had risen up stories high on each side. It felt even darker that it had in the open.

Knowing the ghost town was up ahead somewhere, he wondered how far the walls would continue on either side of him. Dragon stopped dead. *What was that?* He heard something in the distance, and after listening for moment realized it was a train. He looked forward and back.

"Ai ya!" *Shit.*

He turned around and ran back to the beginning of the rock cut, jumping off the rails. He landed roughly and ended up sitting on the gravel shoulder wide-eyed and breathing hard. Dragon's heart beat against his ribs and he felt the cold sweat of fear. It wasn't something he was used to.

He thought the train had been right on top of him, but now he couldn't hear it at all. Then it was there again. He scrambled up and stumbled off the main rail line onto the siding. The sound was louder, but still fading in and out.

He took a few breaths and tried to calm himself, the ground started to shake as the train finally roared out of the rock cut. The big headlight bore through the darkness, bright enough to cause Dragon to raise his arm, covering his eyes.

He felt himself back-peddling even farther from the track as the pounding roar of the steel wheels exploded out of the cut and the train went racing by. Dragon was looking both ways, not sure if he wanted to watch the front of the train as it disappeared away from him, or keep watching the cars coming through the cut. In his head somewhere he was being told to not take his eyes off any of it and he backed up further.

The shaking ground and the screech of steel on steel added to his confusion and suddenly the last rail car went by and the sound faded even more quickly than it began. Dragon watched the blinking red light on the end of the train disappear in the distance. He stood there and let the comfort of the silence return.

When he felt back in control he continued his walk, staying out in the open area and away from the rock cut. That was definitely not a place to be at night. In the dark he almost missed the little road at the back of the hill. He remembered that they used horses back then to travel an old road that went around the back of the hill into the town.

Dragon's plan called for walking straight down the tracks to the old ghost-town and hadn't included using the old road. He'd forgotten about it. Now he looked into the darkness wondering if he should check it out. He was ten minutes up the trail when he heard something in the woods.

What was that? Dragon thought about his gun for the first time and realized that walking around in the dark in a strange place wasn't a good idea. He decided to give it up for the night. Heading back down the trail he noticed the shipping container.

He couldn't believe he'd walked right past it on the way in. He couldn't help going to the doors and shaking the chain. He examined the padlock and wondered what was stored inside.

Dragon was thinking about the riddle as he walked back to the join the others. "Big tongue in the water, protected by two. What do you mean by that Tiger?"

He switched his thoughts to Tiger. His great-grandfather had worked this very land. Hopefully he had found something to make the sacrifice worth it.

Dragon started to laugh when he got back to the trailer. Li had given the workers some blue plastic tarps and they had set up makeshift tents to sleep in. He realized he hadn't been thinking about that stuff, and Li obviously wasn't interested in sharing the trailer.

He knew it would be cold overnight, it was well into the fall, but he was counting on the temperatures making the workers eager to work to warm up when needed. Inside the trailer he found Li sitting back with a beer. "I see you've taken care of the workers."

"They're lucky to get tarps," the two men laughed together.

Yes, they should be happy with what they have, he thought, because if the solution to the riddle proved lucrative there may be little chance they leave here alive.

CHAPTER 10

West of Jackfish, 1883

The workers were worn down by the effort required to carve through the rock along the north shore. Tiger had doubled the number of men he was letting take a day off and hide in the woods, but it wasn't enough. This section of rail was the hardest they'd done yet.

His crews didn't get any help from railcars that could have provided cranes or power drills. They continued to do all their work by hand. The movement of boulders and tons of gravel was endless.

The bosses were spending more time up at the front with the Chinese crews now that they had slowed down and Tiger was constantly answering for their lack of progress. He knew he was under attack and that his control was slipping.

The first problem had been with the food. Somehow the food had been tampered with one night and all the workers were sick. The work ground to a halt the next day as his men struggled to work without falling over.

They all passed it off as a coincidence, but when it happened again three days later, the second time in a week,

Tiger realized it was more than chance. That bastard Meng was trying to undermine him.

The second time it happened the workers became upset and started questioning what was going on. Tiger knew he was the one who was taking the brunt of the accusations. Couldn't he protect the basics, like the food? He assigned one of his half dozen most trusted soldiers to stay with the cook during food preparation and the last number of days things had gone well.

Secondly, some of the workers started showing up bruised and beaten at morning call. It turned out the camp was now no longer safe for Chinese after dark. Naturally, the rumblings were becoming regular; fear levels were rising.

He still had a hold over the men, but Meng was chipping away at the edges and Tiger knew his opponent was gaining ground. Meng had the advantage of a gang of twenty hardened criminals. With only his six soldiers, the five hundred workers were up for grabs. Meng was clearly going for it. It was only a matter of time before he would be talking with the bosses and applying pressure. He would be blaming Tiger for the slowdowns and trying to convince them that the workers were no longer following his leadership.

While he knew that the progress had stalled due to terrain and sickness, neither of which were his fault, appearances were everything and progress was the only factor of importance. He kept the word flowing to his men to watch out for the criminals and reminded them of their strength in numbers, but word kept coming back that they wanted protection. The protection they were paying for.

*****

The rain was enough to soak a man to the bone. The day had been a long wet struggle to move tons of rock. The men were all hunched over, shivering and tired. They marched back to camp for food and rest. Tiger could hear the uproar before he got there.

Murmurs rose to a roar, then he could hear shouts of anger and disbelief. There were hundreds of men to push through and he took a while getting through the growing crowd.

As he neared the front he could see men bunched together, trying to see over each other.

"*Shan kai!* Get out of the way. Move."

Tiger pushed through the human wall until he was standing alone in front of the crowd. They had gathered there in the middle of the camp staring at the sight on the ground. Two bodies, the cook and the soldier he had left on guard, were sprawled out on the ground, hacked to pieces.

Tiger had seen a lot in his time back in the Chinese mountains and even created some horror of his own, but this sight was one he knew he would never forget. The message was going to have the effect his enemies wanted.

The damage looked like it had been done with an axe. The men looked like a puzzle to Tiger. Bones had been broken and sliced apart and no leg or arm looked straight. They were bent and cracked in all directions. The mess around the stomach was ugly with guts hanging out the sides of the bodies. The soldier's head was almost cut off, still attached, hanging to one side by a thread of muscle and skin. The axe must not have gotten the neck cleanly.

Tiger stood in the rain and stared. He was shocked and took a second to compose himself. Things were escalating faster than he'd wished. Now he watched as the pools of blood washed away with the rain, making long red streaks that meandered through the dirt.

The sound of the men grumbling brought him back to his senses. He turned to the group. "Enough of this whining. Food will be cooked soon, you will all eat later. Now go and rest."

He waved the crowd away from the scene, keeping only his soldiers and a few workers. "Get these two men out of here." The soldiers dragged away the bodies.

He pointed at the workers. "You men start to make a dinner. Use what you can and make soup for everyone." The workers stared back blankly and Tiger jumped towards them. "Now." He was angry enough that they realized there was a chance of getting hurt and quickly moved towards the cook fire.

With the situation under control he headed back to his own tent. He found it empty and lifeless without Bao, he still wasn't over what he had done. He knew why he'd done it, but wondered if he'd ever get over it.

He had talked with the white men who worked ahead of his crews laying the stakes and choosing the route. He was trying to decide where he could get off the railway. They had mentioned their route would take them close to the water again soon. Tiger knew his choices were limited to ship or rail, to try and walk out of these woods would be suicidal. He could walk back the way the rail had come, but that was still endless miles of wilderness.

Knowing the situation with Meng was only going to get worse, he realized he couldn't wait any longer.

*****

The five soldiers and their leader worked their way quietly through the woods. They had purposely gone into the bush, taking the long way to go around everything, staying out of sight. Tiger knew that the last group of arrivals were working clean-up behind the rail line as it moved forward.

They would smooth the gravel and landscape the ditches and be the last to touch each area. He also knew that their tents would be back somewhere past where they were working. The newcomers were stuck tagging along at the back of the procession.

Tiger and his men worked their way around the tent area, keeping to the woods until they were well past the sleeping men. Now they approached from the ditch along the new rail line, up behind the quiet camp. Meng was cocky and confident, and Tiger hoped that meant the man wasn't expecting any trouble. He was sure that Meng thought his opposition was an easy target.

They held up outside the camp and waited. Their plan called for one of the gangsters to make the mistake of coming out for a late night piss. When one finally showed up, it was the last one he had. He never had a second to yell, his pants were down during the attack and he was more worried about his jewels than calling for help.

He was quick to answer Tiger's questions, as would anyone with a knife held to their member. The man was rather concerned about the knife and kept looking down at it. He didn't have to worry about his jewels, they didn't matter after his neck was slit from side to side.

Tiger stepped over the body and continued on with his plan. He now had the information he needed, and with just one of the soldiers at his side, he ventured into the maze of tents. The others held their positions and waited for their boss.

Stepping like a shadow, with his senses on full alert, Tiger crept up to the tent he was looking for. Life was full of gambles and this was a big one. If the tent was the wrong one, or the man got a shout out, then it would be all over. There would be no escaping this camp, even in the darkness.

He knew that Meng was capable, but was sure that the gangster was toughest with his men around him. Tiger had spent months on his own in the mountains and fought by himself for his family. He didn't need men surrounding him to make him feel strong. He only brought them along to do the dirty work, it was that simple.

When it came to something strategic he wanted done, he did it himself. With a last look around in the rain, he steeled himself and stooped to enter the tent. In under a tick of a second he confirmed that he was in the right place.

He would have liked to take his time and really explore this man's capacity for pain, just for the aggravation and harm he was causing. It would have been a slow death in his mountains, but here there was too much at stake, including Tiger's life.

Moving swiftly over to the cot, he held his hand hovering just above Meng's mouth and brought the knife up close to the man's neck. There was going to be some pleasure in this act, and enjoyment of the surprise. Tiger let himself smile.

Clamping his hand down hard onto the gangster's mouth he watched his victim's eyes burst open. He leaned in, ensuring his body weight was holding the criminal down as the trashing began. Tiger placed the tip of the knife roughly up against Meng's neck, pushing. The thrashing stopped as the criminal realized the position he was in. Tiger watched him trying to focus his eyes and saw the moment when he realized who was holding him down.

There was the anger he'd been waiting for and as the snarl spread across Meng's face Tiger leaned forward. "You die like a dog, lost in a foreign land and never remembered." He rammed the knife in and watched his opponent's face contort as Tiger twisted the blade and thrust it side to side. He held on until his victim stopped moving and the body went limp. Pulling the knife out, he wiped off the blood on Meng's blanket.

He felt the moment of triumph. Tiger soaked it in, feeling the power surging through his body. He stared down and let the sight burn into his brain. It would sit there with all the others that Tiger had stored. This one felt good though, his opposition had been ruthless and worthy, and he let himself relax and enjoy the victory even though he knew he should leave.

His man standing guard outside the tent was still waiting and the two of them quickly re-joined the others at the back of the encampment.

As they worked their way back through the woods to their own camp, Tiger was hoping that cutting off the head of the snake had solved his problem.

*****

Things had settled down on the railroad. Tiger had written his letter and gotten it into the hands of one of the bosses. He was sure it would make it back to China.

There was something about the autumn in this damned north and the rains that wouldn't give an inch, that made it hard to get the work done. They were nearing the end of another hard day while the rain came down constantly. Tiger was up ahead checking the next section of terrain when one of his men came running. "Tiger, there's a problem back in the pit."

The pit was a large hole they were trying to dig in soft material so they could refill it with stable rock. The bosses decided they had to dig down into the swampy area until they were through the muck and found hard ground underneath. As he walked back he noticed some of the men gathering around the edge of the hole, looking down into it.

Tiger stopped at the top, at first he was shocked at how deep it was. They had gone much further down that he had planned. *Why?* They had gone past the swamp bottom and started digging in harder ground. He was further shocked by the mess of men jostling in the bottom of the pit, yelling and punching each other. *What the hell was going on?*

Tiger looked around the pit and couldn't see any of his soldiers. He wanted to send them down to sort it out. With no one left, it fell to him and he instructed the soldier who had come to find him in the first place to follow him into the pit. The two men stepped over the lip and started down into the wet muddy hole.

Once he was on the bottom and looking back at the top he realized that the hole was at least twenty feet deep instead of stopping at the ten-foot mark where the ground became hard. Tiger didn't notice some of the workers climbing out of the hole as he started to question the others.

"Why are you digging this deep? What has come over you men?"

No one answered, but more men started to climb up the slippery sides of the hole.

"Answer me you idiot," Tiger screamed at a worker who stared back blankly.

The laughing from above caught Tiger's attention and he looked up. The top of the hole was now ringed with men. He noticed for the first time that most of the workers had left the hole. He was left there with his soldier and the two workers he was yelling at.

"We have decided we no longer want to work for you Tiger, the great leader." The last words were said with disgust. In the pouring rain he couldn't make out the face of the man who was challenging him from above.

"Who are you to challenge me? Come down here and show yourself."

The laughing continued in a voice full of contempt. "You have no say. You are now nobody. You have messed with the wrong family and now we'll finish it."

Tiger did nothing as the last two workers were called out of the pit. He thought about his mistake. He hadn't done proper research on Meng. He had never even thought about the possibility the man had relatives in the gang.

Once he had shown his hand and attacked the gang, they had obviously worked behind the scenes to create this scenario. They had staged it all and now he realized why the hole was so deep. As Tiger looked up he focused on the speaker, the man stepped back from the edge and yelled out, "Finish the hole!"

Tiger didn't react, he was a proud man. The soldier with him wasn't as strong and he started trying to climb out. The workers standing around the top of the hole started shovelling dirt and pushing rocks down into the pit. First it was a boulder and some gravel to dodge and then they all started pushing rocks over the edge. Tiger caught sight of his soldier out of the corner of his eye as the man neared the top of the hole.

Someone lifted a large rock and threw it at the soldier. The boulder hit him on the head and drove him off the wall. He tumbled back towards the bottom as Tiger dodged boulders, trying to avoid rocks coming at him from every direction.

Something large hit his back. The heavy weight drove him forward. His head slammed down against another boulder. He rolled to the side and sat up. The blood running into his eyes told him his head was cut open. He yelled out as another boulder rolled down the bank bouncing over smaller rocks before landing hard and pinning his legs.

He laid down on the rough rock and looked up at the sky. The rain was filled with large objects and he forced himself to be quiet as the rocks hit his chest and head. Trying to keep his eyes open he focused on the sky but one eye was damaged from a direct hit and then his vision was blocked out as the rocks began to pile over him.

Tiger thought of home and his mountains. The weight of the increasing pile of rock was making it hard to breathe. He smiled to himself and let pride flow through his weakened body. He wondered what the date was.

His family would be set for generations.

CHAPTER 11

Terrace Bay, 2012

With the cruiser parked back behind the station and her reports done, April jumped in her pick-up and headed home. The old house on the edge of town had been handed down to her. There weren't a lot of out of town properties, and she was glad to have one of them.

She was tired today and wondering about that guy down at Jackfish as she pulled in the driveway. *Aw, Christ. Not again.* She saw the pick-up and her heart sank. What the fuck was he doing here this time?

She couldn't see Brad anywhere as she rolled to a stop beside his truck, ensuring he had plenty of room to leave. Then she noticed the light on inside her house and got concerned. Should she call for backup?

She didn't carry a gun off duty and her own rifle was locked up in the house. She had to go in sooner or later, and readied herself to step out of her truck.

"Brad Harrison, are you in there?"

The front door burst open and he stumbled out with a beer in his hand. "We need to talk."

"I don't think so. We've got nothing to say." It had been two years since she had booted him out, although it should have happened years earlier. She needed to get the dammed lock changed. In the back of her head she knew she hadn't because it would just piss him off enough he'd break down the door anyway.

"You bitch. I know you still want me. You still have my name. Let's have some fun for old time's sake."

She'd meant to start that damn process a number of times and was always too busy with something else. She'd finally gotten around to the paperwork, it was already sent in and all she was doing was waiting. She wouldn't be using his name much longer.

"Brad, you need to get out of here. You're drunk, and me calling the cops would be a bad thing for you."

"Hey, you do what you got to. I'm going to do whatever I feel like. It's not over yet honey."

"Yes, Brad, it is. Has been for years." She realized she pushed it too far as his eyes went hard.

"We both know you aren't seeing anybody. You'll be back," he waved his beer at her. "Besides, you see someone around here and I'll kill them. And you know it."

"Are you leaving, or am I calling?"

He stepped off the deck and walked towards her. April kept the truck between them as he laughed at her.

"When you come asking for it baby, I'm really going to give it to you." He jerked his truck door open and slid behind the wheel. As he put the pick-up in reverse he smiled at her. "See you soon sexy."

April watched the truck back out onto the road. This was never going to end. She wondered if the reason she wasn't seeing anybody was because she knew he had been telling her the truth. She ought to just report him, but she didn't want to be seen as using her position to solve a personal problem.

It really was simple, she was going to have to deal with Brad sooner or later and bring things to a conclusion. But there was no way it wasn't going to be messy.

Book 2
Discovery

CHAPTER 12

The sun wasn't up yet, but Phil was. When the fish were running you tried to capitalize on it. He was gearing up for another three-hour walk east to the Steel River. It looked like a nice day was coming and the early bird always got the fish.

The morning light was starting to break through the darkness as he wound his way down the trail along the back of the hill and around to the tracks. He was on autopilot this morning. Too many drinks the night before had put him out early and he was still a little groggy.

He was trudging along, head down, when instinct kicked in. Something was out of the ordinary, so he stopped and straightened up. He was almost at the east of the siding, near the gravel road up to the highway.

He looked slowly around in a three hundred and sixty degree circle and came to rest on the camper and truck that must have pulled into the open area during the night. No lights, but it was still early. Phil relaxed and let the muscles in his neck unwind themselves.

Just travellers who would be gone later when he got back. With a long walk ahead, Phil wasn't wasting any time on them. He pointed his head forward and continued down the rail line.

*****

When Dragon opened his eyes he was already excited, knowing his quest was going to be over soon. Wondering what was waiting at the end, he didn't care, he was just glad that he'd found the place.

No one was around, it was perfect. They got the workers busy gathering some wood. Then him and Li went exploring. They headed right back to the far end of the siding where Dragon had seen the hill and rock cut. He knew the ghost town was supposed to be in that direction.

Stopping at the entrance to the rock-cut, the two men looked along the track and then up at the shear walls of dark granite framing the rail line. Dragon listened hard trying to make sure he didn't hear anything. Li was listening even harder. He had heard the story of the night before.

Finally, sure it was clear, they ventured into the shadows of the cut. There was less rock on the water side, the walls kept climbing the further into the rock canyon they went. At the halfway point the walls were seven or eight stories high on the inland side and three or four on the water side. You didn't want to meet a train here.

Both men were lost in their own thoughts. Dragon was imagining creating this squared opening. The rock that had been taken out was nowhere to be found, it must have been moved somewhere else.

As they came out of the cut they stopped and looked back. It was something new to them. You sure didn't see anything like that in the Chinese mountains. A little further along they came to the first signs of the old railway station.

The concrete base of the old water tower was still there, standing twenty feet off the track on the hill side. It would have provided water for the steam engines. Dragon ignored the mess of concrete and rebar left crumbled and tangled on the water side of the tracks, it didn't seem relevant to the riddle.

The pictures he had looked at in his research were still clear in his mind. He recognized the old derelict building sitting on a point of rock near the water as the old stationmaster's house. His job had been to manage the coal and water for the trains and receive the ships bringing in supplies.

Dragon and Li kept moving forward until they began to notice the remnants of an odd building here and there squashed into the low spot between the tracks and the hillside.

A cove on the water side past the station house opened into a nice sandy beach. Dragon let his eyes continue down the beach to the end. He knew the fishing village had been down there, their docks jutting out from the shore. There was no sign of them now.

The tattered buildings in the hollow were starting to multiply as Dragon and Li came across the remains of an ancient car. The rust had eaten right through the frame and bushes were growing out the empty windows.

"You haven't told me why we are here Dragon."

No he hadn't. He had said they were going on a long trip and that had been enough for Li, at least until now.

"This is the middle of nowhere. Is there a purpose to this?" His friend kept pursuing his line of thought.

Everything has a purpose. Yours Li, is to be a trusted soldier. Mine is to expand a family empire. "Yes, Li there is a purpose, you'll see soon enough. Trust me."

Li nodded. That was good enough for him.

Finally they came to the town. The few houses still standing suggested it had all been built on the hillside facing the water, the tracks dividing it from the beach. They couldn't help checking out one of the old shacks. "Look how small the house is Li. We would have to bend over to walk around inside."

Dragon didn't know why they were so small. He didn't think the people were that short, so it must have been because of a shortage of supplies. But that didn't make much sense as he looked at the surrounding forest. Maybe small was easy to heat.

At one time there were three hundred men working to unload coal from the ships. It would have been a busy town. Now there weren't many buildings left, but the base of the schoolhouse still existed. The biggest thing remaining was the footings of what had been a hotel.

Dragon had actually been fascinated with the stories that surrounded the old hotel. Built in the late eighteen hundreds, it had been a mainstay on the north shore for almost eighty years. Three stories high, there was even a pool table on one of the upper floors. Fights in the tavern often poured out into the front yard from the hundred foot long bar.

Dragon didn't know much history, but the book said that King George the fifth and Queen Elizabeth had stayed there in 'thirty-nine, he assumed they were important. He found it interesting that there had been Japanese prisoners of war held in the area during World War Two and that the guards were billeted at the hotel, making the journey to the prison camp each day by train.

He hadn't understood what the big deal was about a group of seven painters who had stayed there on and off over the years until he checked their paintings out and realized they were now considered pretty famous. He wondered since they had been there so often, if any of their paintings been lost in the fire that took the place down and finally killed the town.

In the end the only history that mattered to him was Tiger's. Dragon pulled out the sheet of paper with the riddle and took a long deep breath.

He had already figured out the first lines, or hoped he had, especially the Jackfish part.

Come to the land of tree and rock,

Simple people, land of riches, a fish named Jack.

Now he was looking at the next lines to determine what to do.

Big tongue in the water, protected by two,

Walking steel eyes into the late day sun, past the two,

This was where he had to get his brain working. It mentioned the water, so he headed away from the hotel out to the beach. Standing on the rocky shore he thought about a big tongue in the water and it hit him. The ships. They would have needed a big dock.

There were pictures before and after the landing was built. They had walked right past that mess of crumbled concrete which must have been the footings for the long dock.

Dragon stood at the very edge of the lapping waves and imagined the dock stretching out into the lake. Was that the big tongue? He turned and looked back towards the ghost town, trying to see what the protecting two was supposed to be. The old houses and burnt out hotel offered nothing. Trying to be patient, he pushed back his annoyance and stared up at the sky. He wished the dock was still there because he wanted a better vantage point to look at the landscape.

He was about to look back down when he noticed that the hill behind the town was actually two hills that flowed together like the humps on the back of a camel. Dragon's hands shook a bit at the realization.

Big tongue in the water, protected by two.

He was standing exactly where he was supposed to be.

He was riveted on the piece of paper, looking at the next line that spoke of *steel eyes*. Standing there on the beach looking down he knew there was no steel under his feet. He ignored Li who was becoming impatient with standing around.

Climbing up towards the raised track he realized there was only one type of steel here. As he stared down at the track he pondered; he knew that the two stood for the hills, the late day sun would be setting in the west, so he turned that way and stared. Tiger must have been searching for a way to describe the place and yet keep it confusing. He supposed that the steel rails were like eyes to them back then, because it determined where they went and they were always looking ahead as they laid the rails down.

Follow the railway line past the two hills into the late-day sun.

He couldn't believe it was that simple, but luck worked in mysterious ways. It was only noon and he decided to wait until later to walk the tracks when the setting sun was present like the riddle called for. He might miss something if he looked now, and his gut told him to follow the riddle like Tiger wanted.

"We're close Li, real close." He didn't look to see if Li responded, he was wondering what Tiger had found. He could almost see his great-grandfather standing there, pointing west along the tracks.

*****

Phil walked back home from a good day on the river with a bag of fish slung over his shoulder. The warm afternoon sun was beating down. He had forgotten about the campers, only remembering them as he approached the clearing at the siding.

The memory made him slow down as he looked for the camper. It was still there, he came to a complete stop.

"Okay."

He watched from his vantage point, seeing four men and then another joined them from inside the trailer, so at least five. Not a travelling family or a couple. Hunters maybe? Something made Phil want to stay out of sight, so he considered his options: he needed to get to the other side of the clearing and up onto his hill. But following the tracks across the big opening was out of the question.

He looked down at the lake. That would do. Stepping off the track down into the ditch, he aimed for the thin tree line separating the beach from the rail. Following a path through the trees he came out at the waterside. If he walked the beach, which was lower than the tracks above, they wouldn't see him. Then Phil spotted the guy.

He seemed to be packing up. There was a blanket folded near his feet and he was closing up a lawn chair. The little rubber dingy on shore was completely out of scale with the large lake. Where had the guy come from? Phil looked around confused, then literally jumped back a step when he saw a long gray thing laying out in the water.

His eyes said it was a submarine, but his brain wouldn't acknowledge it. He turned back to the man who was getting ready to leave. Phil's opportunity to satisfy his curiosity was slipping away.

Keeping one hand on the rifle sling, he took a few more steps forward. The guy finally noticed Phil, turning to greet him with a big smile. "Hey there, what's up?"

"I was going to ask you the same thing,"

"A little tanning before the weather turns."

"You come here often?" Phil couldn't believe the stupid words, as the line came out of his mouth. It sounded like a bizarre pick-up line.

"I've been coming up here for years, love it here."

Phil nodded towards the submarine. "You live on that thing?"

"Yeah. I've been doing that for years too." The guy laughed.

"Where did you come from?" He realized he was drilling the guy.

"I was down in the Caribbean. But I'm usually all over the place."

Phil looked out at the thing he knew was a submarine. It appeared to be made of concrete. Only a hundred yards off shore, he could see it clearly. He really didn't know what to say next. Swinging the fish bag off his shoulder he undid the top. Reaching in, he looked at the traveller.

"You want a fish?" He pulled one of them out of the bag.

"You bet Batman. Thanks a lot." He added the fish to the rest of his stuff and pushed the dingy into the water.

Phil held the little boat steady as the man climbed in. As he let go his visitor started to paddle away. He yelled back at Phil. "Where you living?"

"Here at Jackfish."

Phil watched the guy's face change slightly, as he took a minute to respond. "Really? Well maybe I'll see you again sometime."

Phil had no answer to that. He watched the guy load his stuff into the top hatch of the sub and climb in. He couldn't move. He just stared as the sub started to move slowly, turning out towards the center of the lake. When it started to slip lower in the water, disappearing, he kept staring.

"Did that just happen?"

He looked at the footprints on the beach and knew it had, but Jesus. When his brain finally kicked back to the campers, he turned and started to walk home, but kept staring back at the water.

He wanted to get on top of the hill. He needed the higher elevation to really get a look at what was going on with those men outside the trailer. Putting the submarine out of his mind, he finally picked up his pace.

CHAPTER 13

April Harrison sat in her cruiser on the side of the highway and let the radar do its thing. Usually, she leaned back against the reclined seat and rested. Unless the speeder's reading was off the chart, she ignored them.

She didn't become a cop to drive people's insurance costs through the roof. She didn't even think the two things should be connected.

Up here you had miles of straight road and hours between towns. The old "moose and spruce" scenario. She couldn't help but speed herself when she was going from point A to B. That went a long way towards her letting off the marginal ones. She didn't like bad guys or crooks though. She'd become a cop to get a good job and pension and had expected a lot of the shit that came with the job, but at least felt she would be doing the right thing and fighting for the good.

After the years she'd spent in this quiet area it had settled into being just a job.

She was thinking about the new guy who was supposed to be down at Jackfish. She seemed unable to tamp down her curiosity. She didn't like having questions filled with unknowns.

A car pulled off the highway, up beside her cruiser and she quickly moved her seat back to its upright position. April slid her window down.

"Hello Officer, are we on the road to Sudbury?" The wife smiled at her from the passenger seat.

"Yes, you are." It was everything she could do not to laugh. "It's another nine hours east."

April watched the disappointment cross their faces. The TransCanada Highway was a long affair, and here in the north it was hours of rock, hill, and bush that literally went on and on. This couple was obviously getting tired of the trek.

"Oh dear," the woman responded. "We've still got a ways to go. Thank you."

Watching the car leave, she noticed the British Columbia plates. April could see that it was becoming a long trip for the pair of them.

She checked the time, two in the afternoon. She wanted to go back down to Jackfish earlier than the last time. She might have to walk up the hill. With the decision made, she turned around and headed out of town.

You couldn't beat the scenery around here and April always enjoyed the drives. No traffic, some wildlife, and Lake Superior all along the south side of the highway. She looked at one of the few hotels along this stretch as she flew by. More cars and trucks in the parking lot than during the summer months, but it was autumn, and hunting season was coming fast.

That was a crazy time of year, with guns and booze in the woods. It never failed that something went wrong once you put those two things together. She shook it off, moose season hadn't started yet and there was no sense getting worked up about things before she needed to.

Ten minutes past the hotel, at the gravel road, she turned right heading down the hill towards the rail siding. Since the CP crews said they'd seen him along the tracks maybe she'd catch him out walking around. She was trying to decide if she should drive around or park and walk. She was almost down to the open area when she noticed the camper trailer. It hadn't been there the other day. It was probably a traveller looking to take a break and get away from the transport trucks roaring along the highway. Wouldn't they be surprised when the first train went past in the middle of the night.

Slowing to get a good look was just part of being alert and on the job. There were two simply dressed Chinese men who looked normal enough, piling wood at the back of the trailer. The entrance door and what seemed to be a sitting area under the awning faced away from the road towards the forest. She nodded at the two men who smiled back as she drove past. After driving by, curious, she made sure to angle the cruiser so that she could watch in her side mirror and get a look at the sitting area on the other side.

Even in the side-mirror the tattoos of the men sitting at the table under the awning were clear. She only thought for a second before stepping on the brake pedal and shifting into park. Something about these guys had made her stop, she didn't know what.

She opened the door, keeping her eyes trained on the two men. They weren't moving, which was always a good sign. She stood there and assessed the situation. Those two looked a lot more troubling than the wood stackers.

When the first one stood and took a step towards her, she instinctively moved her hand to her waist, but tried to keep things casual. "Hello, everything all right with you folks?"

From the confusion on his face she assumed he didn't understand her. She didn't like the way his eyes had gone up and down her body either. He turned and yelled at one of the other men in a foreign language. One of the wood stackers at the back of the trailer came running forward.

Okay, that cleared up one question. This guy was giving orders to the others. The new man addressed her, "Hello, can I be of assistance?"

"I was just asking this guy if everything was all right here."

"Yes, everything is good, no problem."

"You didn't even tell him what I said. Tell him now." She wondered about that. Why hadn't he told the guy in charge? What had the boss said to the man in the first place? *Get rid of her?*

She watched him translate and then a smile spread across the face of the guy in charge. He spoke to his man and April was told that indeed everything was fine.

"So where are you going?"

This time the man translated immediately. "Take a break and then continue to Toronto."

"Vacation?"

"Yes, we have family there, a sister getting married."

The whole time the conversation was going on April hardly looked at the guy speaking to her. She kept her eyes going back and forth under her sunglasses tracking the boss man and the character still sitting at the table. He'd been staring at her intently since she climbed out of the truck.

He looked like he was wound up tight and about to spring loose. For some reason she was absolutely sure this man was deadly. He was one of the ones who couldn't hide their true nature. They have a menacing air and carry themselves with confidence. He'd clearly seen violence.

"So how many of you are there?"

"Six of us." She watched the leader laugh and then got the translation. "Too many."

She smiled at the joke, but her brain was going full speed. What to do? There really wasn't anything out of the ordinary, and tattoos in themselves weren't a problem. But her instincts were saying something was up.

"Well, good luck with your trip." She waited for a thank you before nodding and turning to walk away. At the truck she turned back before climbing in, the men were still standing there watching her departure. No one had moved. That didn't sit well with her either. Didn't people who were innocent just go about their business? Why were these guys standing there like statues?

Driving out into the clearing she remembered the guy on the hill and looked up. Was that another reflection? She wasn't going to climb up there right now with those campers back there. She hadn't gotten a good vibe from them at all.

Suddenly the radio in the cruiser came to life, she had a call. There was an accident on the highway just out of town. Some cyclist had been hit by a vehicle. Well, she surely wasn't hiking up the hill now. She turned the truck around and headed back along the tracks.

She couldn't help slowing down as she went past the camper again and noticed that no one was outside. Where had they gone? Were all six of them sitting inside? Why? She would have to come back down here to check out the wild man and make sure these campers had moved on.

*****

As the cop drove away Dragon was yelling, "Get everything packed up, now!"

He'd been shaken by their visitor. A cop. A female on top of that. Her looks had him left reeling. He hadn't seen a lot of women since they'd arrived in Canada, they hadn't taken the time to hit the bars or strip joints where he usually found companionship. This one was simply gorgeous. The look on her face and her body language when she was ready to pull out her gun said she was to be taken seriously.

He'd never thought of women as dangerous, but that one was. "We'll move the trailer into the woods. We don't want that again."

"Oh, I'm not so sure Dragon, did you see the body on that one?" Li smiled. He had been ready to jump at her from his chair, even throwing his knife on the way, if she'd come much closer. But she'd managed to avoid that mistake.

"Damn it Li, that was close."

"Yes, I know. She just needed to take a few more steps."

Dragon stared at Li, he knew the soldier was serious. No threat was too big for the man and he was probably getting restless.

With the trailer secured and ready to go, Dragon led them towards the hill and then a bit further along the little road that went around behind. He slowed as he inched into the woods past the container. After walking a bit of the trail the night before, he assumed he could drive it.

When they came to a steep section of trail that was partially washed out, he figured that was far enough. Looking around for a spot to put the camper off the trail, he managed to back the rig into a little clearing between two big trees.

After the others got out he sat in the truck for a few minutes and tried to settle his nerves. He could tell from the look on the cop's face that she had not liked seeing them. He was so close to solving the riddle and couldn't afford any problems with her. She would do well to stay away because he knew that Li would welcome some time with her.

Walking around the trailer he decided this would have to be their camp for now. "Cut down some of this brush and make a bigger clearing. Set up the table and get this place organized," he ordered.

Reaching forward, he slapped two of the workers hard. He stepped closer and knocked one to the ground with a punch. "Get moving!" He was just as restless as Li. They were both used to constant danger in the mountains back home and this extended period of inactivity was getting to him.

Dealing with that cop, added to the time it had taken to move and resettle, Dragon knew it was almost dark and he had to hurry to get back to solving the riddle before he lost all the light. "I'm taking a short walk, I'll be back."

As he headed down the hill past the container and back down towards the railroad track, he kept picturing the good-looking cop and her long blond hair. There weren't too many blondes back home.

Moving quickly down the track, Dragon headed west of the ghost town watching for the next section of the riddle to make sense;

Leaving the ocean, finding the other side of three.

He had waited too long and the fading sun was making it hard to see. The two had referred to the two hills so a third should also be a hill. And sure enough there was another one further along the track beside the two that framed the town. Leaving the ocean and finding the other side of the third hill. Tiger must have meant to go behind this hill but with darkness coming fast he wouldn't see anything now. Tomorrow, he said to himself, tomorrow for sure.

*****

Phil had been poised at the top of the hill leaning over the scope for hours with only a few slight breaks to move and relax his muscles. By the time he had gotten set up there wasn't much movement down at the trailer.

He wished the awning and door of the trailer were facing his way, instead of away from him. He wasn't in a hurry and would wait until he saw something.

Finally a couple guys started to pile wood at the back of the trailer. There was nothing out of the ordinary. Two guys, one in shorts, the other in jeans. They seemed to be in their late twenties. The wood meant they were staying at least the night. Again he thought, maybe early hunters.

"No threat there."

He lowered the scope, about to give up on them and start thinking dinner when he noticed something out of the corner of his eye. A dust cloud was coming down the gravel road. He couldn't see the vehicle yet behind the trees. Then he caught sight of the black and white of an OPP cruiser.

"Here we go."

Phil watched the cruiser slow down as it neared the trailer. He was intrigued when it came to a stop just past the camper. What had the cop seen? He watched as the cruiser door opened and swung the scope back to his eye.

"Shit."

It was the same female officer as before. What was she doing here again so soon? Idly, he noticed that she looked as good as the last time. When she started to walk towards the trailer and then stopped with her hand moving towards her side arm, Phil focused in.

He swung the scope towards the trailer but still couldn't see anything. Swinging back to the officer he watched her from the side. She was alert, her back stiff as she leaned slightly forward. He could tell she was concerned about something. Phil clicked off the safety and slid his finger around the trigger.

He swung the sights back to the trailer and this time caught sight of two men. One was the Chinese from the back of the trailer but the second was someone entirely new. Phil felt his heartbeat jump. He knew those marks by sight. Gang tattoos.

"Fuck."

The guy was a criminal, Phil would bet his life on it. It was written all over him. He felt his finger tightening on the trigger and forced himself to calm down.

Easy here, wait it out.

Swinging his sights back and forth between the parties he spotted the moment when the tension relaxed and the officer backed off. When she turned and walked back to the cruiser, he couldn't help but follow her and make sure she got into her truck safely.

He kept the scope on her as she started the truck and drove along the siding towards his hill. When she looked up his way and seemed to register his position with her eyes he realized she had probably see him again because of the damned scope.

"Idiot."

Then she was driving back out along the tracks and past the campers where she seemed to slow again. Phil wondered what that all meant. Why was she coming down here? He hadn't seen a cop all summer and now twice in two days. And now there were gangsters hanging around on top of that.

Phil switched his thoughts back to them, his eyes squinted as his jaw locked tight. He fought to focus, but the tattoos had him all over the place. When he realized there was action going on at the trailer he was forced to bring himself back to the present.

They were tearing down to leave. The wood was thrown in the back of the truck and the men were rushing around. When they started climbing into the vehicle he got a look at them all. There was a second gangster sitting in the front with the one he had already spotted.

Phil wondered why they were in such a rush, especially after the cop had already left. It didn't look good. He thought they were on their way out to the highway, so was surprised when they came in his direction.

Then he became concerned as they turned and began following the washed-out old road along the back side of the hill. He couldn't see them, but followed the progress by ear. He was sure they had to be past his container by now.

He heard the truck revving, the sound of brush moving and small trees breaking. They were parking in the woods. *Why? Who were these guys?* Phil was getting angry now, they were invading his carefully maintained private space, and he was fighting himself to not do something about it. He had been slowly putting his head back together over the past few months and now he felt like it was all starting to come apart.

He was going to have to deal with these guys in the morning. But right now he needed a drink. As he headed back to the shelter he thought about the dark alleyways of the city and the blood on the walls. He knew he would be having more than just one drink.

CHAPTER 14

Terrace Bay, 2012

April pulled into the industrial area of town doing her daily rounds. Next she went down to the beach and around the golf course. She was heading back up towards the main street when she started thinking about the guy at Jackfish. He had to come into town for supplies at some point, so someone must have seen him.

She started with the hardware stores and got lucky at Cebrario's. One of the guys remembered a strange looking fellow who matched her longhaired and bearded description.

"Yeah, he was in here. Got himself some heavy gage fencing and metal posts."

"Anything seem out of the ordinary?"

There was a hesitation. "Well, I remember he paid with all brand-new hundred dollar bills."

"So why's that a big deal?"

"I don't know, but the guy seemed to be looking around like he was worried about somebody seeing him. He did look like he'd just stepped out of the bush, so the new bills seemed odd I guess."

April didn't find it that strange. Around here some people still used the old bank of mattress to hide money, or buried it in a nice safe spot.

"How did he take away the fencing?"

"He had a truck with him."

April continued her rounds and stopped at the only grocery store in town, where she'd assume he'd been in regularly. Sure enough, two of Costa's cashiers, Rose and Shelly, remembered the guy and seemed eager to talk about him.

"Tall, quiet, broad shouldered. Nice looking."

The women seemed to like reliving the memory and April decided to push a little farther. "I thought he was a crazy looking bush-man."

"No, not crazy. Rugged." Shelly sighed. April could tell the women were obviously impressed but weren't going to be much help.

"What did he buy? Can you remember?" By this point she was sure they would.

"Yes—flour, salt, sugar, yeast, and some canned stuff."

"So nothing out of the ordinary?"

"Well, he did spend time in Helen's sewing store." The two women instinctively looked out the window of the grocery towards the shop just up the road. April was sure they had spent some time watching him walk away the last time he was there.

"Thanks ladies."

April walked into Helen's Sewing and quickly came to the conclusion that the man had affected Helen as well.

"That wild man with the long hair and beard, has he been in here?"

"He's certainly not a wild man." Helen stuck her chin up in the air.

"Okay, so he's been in here."

"Certainly."

Was it just her or was she having to pull teeth here. "Okay, so tell me about him."

Helen's face opened up in a smile. "A gentle giant, with those penetrating eyes, and he was very polite."

That was three women out of three. Not bad wild man. "So what was he looking for?"

"He bought some needles and some sewing materials."

Really. She found this interesting. Combined with the hardware supplies it did look like he was settling in for a while.

"So you didn't find this guy threatening?"

"Of course not. I hope he stops by again."

April figured the women at the grocery wouldn't mind either. None of this was doing anything to alleviating her curiosity. She stopped in at the ministry office and both gas stations, but no one remembered him in either place.

She needed to get some lunch and decided to hit the bar in Schreiber to see if there were any new sightings by the CP crews. Then she'd better put in a few hours on the radar gun and get back to the office and finish up the paperwork that had piled up over the last few days.

She hated paperwork.

CHAPTER 15

Phil woke in a sweat, still restless from fighting the nightmares. He'd been flashing back. The tattoos were still on his mind. Shaking his head to clear the morning fog, he remembered the two gangsters in the camper trailer.

"Wake up man."

He jumped up, looking around for his rifle. It was still leaning against the box where he left it the night before. A quick survey of the area told him the machete was beside it.

"Okay."

Phil jammed some dry granola mix into his system and filled his pocket with a handful more. He thought of liquor, but grabbed a water container instead. Standing outside the enclosure he looked at his shelter. Would he be back? You just never knew which way these things would go.

He was dressed in camouflage, with the rifle over his shoulder and the machete strapped to his waist. The black shoe-polish he had applied to his face blended with his dark hair and beard.

It was time.

He could walk right down on them. He had a trail that went right to the container and he knew they weren't far, just a ways up the old road from there. But Phil wanted to observe first, so he took a second trail, the one he had cut along the ridge and through the slight valley between the two hills.

When he had gone far enough to be sure he had passed their location, he stepped into the woods and eased carefully between the trees down the side of the hill. He should run into the old road at the bottom well in front of them. Taking his time he ensured his field of view was clear and that each step was placed carefully.

He stopped and listened, then continued. A sudden movement to his left made him pause, and he wasn't sure if it was relief when he realized it was a moose. It was close to rutting season and the beast might decide he was a challenge. Phil wasn't interested in any aggressive encounters. Crouching down, he let the moose move off into the bush before continuing his approach.

Close to the old road now, glimpsing it through the trees, he wasn't going out there where he could be seen. Staying fifteen to twenty feet off of the road, he worked his way parallel to it.

"Where are ya?" he whispered.

There was a current building inside him. He could feel the adrenaline beginning to pump. Were they here to get him? How did they find him? He reached down and gripped the machete's handle.

"Where are you bastards?"

He realized how much he was raging inside and knew he had to rein it in. His training had taught him that emotion had to be controlled in a fight. Use it, but keep it in check with the brain. The brain had to run the show and allow the body to react instinctively. Phil forced himself to slow his breathing and settle down.

He was moving slowly now, a foot here and then another foot. Crouching down, he offered nothing to the watching eye. Catching the color of the trailer through the trees he moved a few feet higher up the hill as he continued to move parallel to the old road.

When he was finally in line with the camper on the other side of the road, he stopped and sat down resting his shoulder against the trunk of a fallen tree. He could just make out its outline through the trees and could almost pick up a voice or two. He contemplated going in with guns blazing, but checked that thought.

"Easy now."

Phil was still trying to decide what to do when the situation changed. He heard yelling and people moving around. He couldn't understand the language, but someone was giving orders. Then he caught sight of the first and then second gangster walking away from the camper, towards the siding and his container.

He wasn't sure what to do. He could hear the other men near the trailer, but it was the gangsters who concerned him. They might be back shortly and he realized he would have to wait. Stepping out from his concealment now would give him away, and until he was sure what was going on, he wasn't doing that.

After considering his options, he backed up in the woods and started to follow, keeping parallel to them, staying in the trees. He couldn't let them out of his sight.

*****

Dragon was energized by the possibilities as he and Li walked away from the camper and past the storage container.

"Li, today we meet our destiny. Today we find our fortune."

Li looked at his friend without understanding. Dragon smiled and slapped him on the shoulder. "You'll see."

They followed the old road back down the hillside to the train tracks. Everything was aligning for Dragon. They would solve the riddle as a pair, which was good luck. It was the twenty-eighth of the month and that combination of leaving on the eighth, arriving on the eighteenth, and finding the wealth on the twenty-eighth was perfect good fortune.

Almost in a hurry, Dragon led them through the rock cut and past the ghost town. As they walked towards the third hill he stepped off the tracks, thinking of the riddle. He was supposed to find something behind the hill.

Wealth and prosperity, awaits in eights,

the white lightning.

The going got tough as they pushed through the trees and tangled underbrush, working their way along the side of the hill. Dragon forged a path as Li tucked in behind trying to avoid branches slapping back at him.

At some point Dragon decided he was near the back of the hill and stopped to think. He figured he should start searching against the hill, because Tiger hadn't left any directions to find anything that was away from it. The forest was too thick to find something without proper instructions. He tried to picture Tiger.

Looking up he guessed that these trees were older than Tiger's time and that his great-grandfather would never have found anything in this tangled thicket. There must have been some sort of a clearing along the base of the hill, so he started to make his way along the line where the rock outcropping met the forest floor.

After ten minutes of heavy slogging, the forest opened up a bit. The underbrush in this section wasn't as thick and the trees weren't as tall. Dragon focused in on the rocky hillside as he walked along. He watched carefully for anything out of the ordinary.

When he came to the overgrown pile of branches and logs heaped against the hillside he had to stop. This was manmade. The pile leaned against the rock, the wood stacked straight up and down.

Slowly looking around, he noticed that another mound of wood was placed in a small pile on the ground to the left.

"This is the spot Li." Dragon turned in a small circle, taking in the whole forest. "Amazing."

Li wasn't sure what to think, he had followed Dragon into many situations, but this one was strange. He had no response.

Dragon started to move the logs from the pile on the ground and soon had all of them off to the side. He was about to start shovelling when Li stepped forward. "I'll dig."

Moving to the side, he let Li start working on the hole. Dragon was light headed. He had actually found the spot all these years later. What was here? Leaning against the rock wall he watched Li work.

Trying to stop his excitement from getting out of hand, Dragon settled his sights on the wood stacked against the hill. He reached over and pushed against the pile, moving it over. When he thought he saw something, he pushed harder, knocking the entire thing over on its side.

Dragon was shocked. *Shit, this was incredible.* He stared in disbelief, immediately knowing he had a problem. He turned to watch Li as his friend dug further. Dragon moved slowly away from the wall. Standing behind Li, he looked down into the hole. What was he going to do?

They both heard a different sound as the shovel hit something and then they saw the bones. That was the answer, even though he didn't like it. Tiger must have made the same decision and Dragon would have to follow his lead. Could he do it?

There wasn't much time to think, Li had stopped digging and would soon be asking what to do next. Dragon already had his hand on the handle of the machete, pulling it slowly out of its sheath. He realized he was shaking and the pain in his heart had already begun.

He swung the machete.

The steel hit Li in the side of the stomach as he started to turn. Dragon felt the blade sink deep into his friend's side as it dug into the ribs. He watched the shock on Li's face and felt tears on his own. Li was trying to speak and couldn't get his words out clearly. There could be only one question. Why?

Dragon jumped down into the hole, cradling his friend, turning him towards the rock wall. "Do you see Li? Do you see?"

Li's life was flowing out of the open wound as he looked up at Dragon and then towards the wall. His vision had starting to blur but he could see the large streak on the wall as he blinked repeatedly to focus.

Dragon watched as his friend's eyes came back to his. He hoped that Li understood how much he hated to do this. He held his friend in his arms until he was finally gone and then some. Lifetime friendships were hard to lose, and when you were the cause of it, they were hard to bear. He also knew he had no other choice.

Loyalty was based on need. Li had always needed Dragon and his family to ensure he was important and had power. There was no threat of Li taking over Dragon's family, but here in this faraway place, with this discovery, Li could easily kill him and never need him or his family again. It wasn't a chance Dragon could take. Now he just had to deal with the consequences. He sat there and stared at the rock wall for what seemed like hours.

Finally, he kicked himself into gear and pushed Li's body into the hole. He filled it back in and camouflaged the site, then he replaced the wood against the wall, hiding his discovery. He had to decide what to do next. He wasn't sure about showing this to the workers. Maybe this should be a one-man show. He didn't even know who owned the land.

With these things on his mind and the adrenaline pounding through his veins, he headed back out to the tracks and back around the hill towards the trailer.

CHAPTER 16

Phil followed the two Chinese gangsters around the hill and up the tracks. When they went in behind the next hill he knew he couldn't go any further. He couldn't be sure he wouldn't walk right up to them. Returning to hide in the woods by the trailer, he waited for them to show back up.

After a few hours of sitting silently in the brush he was getting restless. He thought of confronting the other Chinese who had stayed with the trailer, but he knew it was the gangsters who he was worried about. Was it a coincidence that they were here? Or were they looking for him?

"Bring it on."

He had to wait until they came back, because he needed to force the situation one way or the other. The waiting was the killer. Time was never his friend and now with too much of it on his hands he was fighting the scenes of his past that kept pushing to the front of his head. Images flickered through his brain. Memories of the acrid smell of gunpowder were so strong he snapped to attention. Phil forced himself not to jump up and shoot something.

When he heard footsteps coming up the trail he rolled his shoulders and unkinked his neck. Noticing that there was only one of them, his nerves ratcheted up another notch. Where was the second guy? Was he sneaking through the bush somewhere?

Watching the criminal head towards the trailer, Phil felt the calmness and patience he was holding onto slip away as his anger pushed to the top. He made a quick decision and went for it. He wasn't the scared type.

He stood and walked towards the intruders. Stopping behind a waist-high bush, just off the road, he confronted the campers. "Hello there! You guys lost?"

He watched the leader damn near jump off the ground at the sound of an unexpected visitor. It seemed like he was searching for the source of the voice. The gangster took a quick look at the others before turning to address the intrusion. Phil could see the guy was trying to assess the danger as his eyes scanned left and right.

Then he saw the look of confusion as the guy spotted him. He had to be wondering who was the mad looking guy in camouflage with black face paint? Where did he come from? Was he a threat?

Phil watched as the gangster yelled at one of the other Chinese.

"What does he want?"

"He asks if we are lost."

"It's none of his business. Tell him we are fine."

Phil stayed locked eye to eye with the gangster as the two Chinese talked. Just the stare-down was enough for him. He had been in enough action to tell this guy was serious and capable. He looked like a thug, but his eyes were calculating.

Without waiting for the answer Phil pressed forward, he didn't need to understand the guy. Just watching his reactions to the questions would be enough.

"So why are you parked so far back in the bush?"

The Chinese translated for the gangster as Phil watched. The guy had to search for an answer, which meant it was a lie. Strike one. That didn't do much to relieve his concerns.

"We are here to experience the wilderness and animals."

Phil almost laughed. The lies were starting to make him angrier, he trembled slightly. "So you're not hiding from that cop?"

Phil watched the gangster's eyes dart at him when he heard the translation. Strike two. The two men held their stare. He saw the moment when the leader switched his attitude from relaxed and smiling to aggressive and cocky as he took a few steps forwards, closing the distance. The gangster spoke to the other Chinese who translated, "Who are you to be so concerned about where I go? What is it to you?"

The guy took another step towards him, almost to the edge of the road. Phil brought the rifle up where the Chinese could see it, cradling it against the front of his body. The gangster stopped, spoke quickly in Chinese, with his eyes on the rifle.

"Well, it's my land and my bush." Phil was smiling, but his clenched teeth showed he wasn't happy. *That's right, I'm the owner. Now you have a problem. One you're losing control over.* The rifle was close and the gangster kept staring at it. *Yes, I know how to use it.*

After a few words back and forth the Chinese translated, "Okay sir, we mean no trouble. We just wanted privacy for a day's rest and we'll be moving on shortly. We are going to Toronto."

Strike three. If the guy could only know that wasn't an answer that was going to settle Phil's nerves. He heard the word Toronto and stared intently at the tattoos. The two went hand in hand in Phil's head. These guys hadn't gone to ground though. No one had jumped for a weapon.

He'd confronted them and was no closer to any answers, but he figured he couldn't really shoot them either. What had they done? He didn't like this guy and had a feeling it was mutual. They seemed to recognize each other's role. He stepped out on the road taking a few strides towards the trailer, keeping the gun cradled in his arm, his finger steady on the trigger.

*****

Dragon watched the man step out onto the dirt road. The machete hanging from his waist stood out. This was someone ready to go hand to hand, that was the only purpose of a machete. The stranger was confident as he stood there and he wondered what it meant. The guy had mentioned the cop. Was he around then? If he had seen that, what else did he see?

He realized his secret might not be safe. This was a serious complication and he resisted the urge to jump at the man, even while he held a gun. He was aware enough to realize what was really bothering him; the fact was that Li wasn't here to help with this stranger. Why had he done it? He knew the answer and would have to suffer the consequences.

Dragon watched the man order him to one side of the road with a nod of his head. So he stepped off into the grass. The stranger walked past, never taking his eyes off his. He watched the man's back as he headed down the old road and around a corner.

This was becoming harder and harder. First it was the cop, now this wild man. Dragon was getting annoyed. He was down to one and that wasn't a good number. Now the cop and the stranger made a pair. That's a good number, but not for him.

Well he wasn't leaving, not when he was so close. He yelled at the workers to pack it up again. They were going in deeper. "Get this place packed up. We move up the road and over the wash-out."

He could hear the grumbling between them and he thought he heard one of them say, "The crazy one's gone, we have nothing to fear."

His frustration was nearing a boiling point as he turned on the workers. He'd done it many times in the mountains. Someone bucked the schedule or shirked a load and thought they were safe in numbers. Dragon had learned that once the first one slowed down the others would slow down as well. No one liked to work harder than the other guy.

The solution was simple. He found that once the group was one man short they always seemed to work harder. Marching towards the man who had opened his big mouth, he rolled his arm around the worker's neck. Already clasping one side of the man's head, the other hand came around from the back and gripped the jaw.

"You're right about one thing. You have nothing left to fear." He jerked his hand, pulling the man's jaw sideways. There was a moment where the neck went tight and couldn't turn anymore. That's when Dragon reefed once more and the neck let go. The cracking was the only sound as the body went limp and he released his grip, letting the dead man slide to the ground.

"Anyone else have any complaints?" He watched the workers busy themselves packing up the trailer. "Good."

They had the trailer out on the road and were ready to take a run at the washed-out track when they heard an engine start in the distance. Bells went off in Dragon's head. Who the hell was that? Where was there another vehicle?

He had a bad feeling, not for the first time today. "Hold on right here, I'll be back in a minute."

CHAPTER 17

Phil drove the highway through Terrace Bay. Sitting in the bush he'd had time to think. He decided it was better to do a hand-off than get involved. He couldn't get a worse vibe than the one he was getting off that Chinese character. That one was hard-core.

Walking away from them on the trail, he'd headed straight for the container. The pins on the doors had been greased exactly for this purpose, a quiet getaway. Releasing the lock he slowly slid the chain free. The two big doors opened without squealing.

The container was purposely raised in the back, which allowed him to get in the pickup, turn the key without starting, and shift into neutral. The truck slowly rolled forward and he guided it out onto the old road. Now he could close the doors and re-chain the lock before he made any noise starting the truck.

Phil pulled into the empty parking lot of the cop station in Schreiber. He should have figured no one would be there. He didn't know how many cops manned this station, but assumed they were all on the road. Recognizing the phone on the side of the building he got out. *For emergency call 1800 555 9934.*

Phil dialled and waited. A cheerful female voice answered, "Hello, April Harrison, Ontario Provincial Police. Can I help you."

"I was hoping to talk with you today if that's all right."

She found that strange. The caller wasn't identifying himself. In this town everyone did.

"Can I ask what this is about?"

"Strange men at Jackfish."

This caught her completely off guard. "And you know this because?"

"Because I live there."

Holy shit. The wild man was calling her. "Can I ask who's speaking?"

"That doesn't really matter. I'm at the station if you have the time."

                              *****

April hung up and threw the SUV in gear, sending gravel spraying as she made a tight U-turn.

Her mind was spinning as she pulled into the station, she had a million questions. The wild man got out of a dusty old pick-up truck to meet her as she climbed out of the cruiser.

"April Harrison." She stuck her hand out.

Phil took the hand. "Call me PH."

She didn't like the answer but decided not to push. It was hard to get a good look at him with the hair and beard. The initials were a stall tactic, but she wasn't in a hurry. "Let's take a seat inside."

She swiped a keycard to unlock the back door of the old white house alongside the highway which had been converted to a police station. Holding the door wide she waved him through, into the cramped common office with its pair of old metal desks pushed together in the center of the room.

She stared at him sitting stone-faced across the desk. She could tell he was fit, strong, even under the rumpled clothes. He seemed very observant, watching her every move as he sat ramrod straight but somehow at ease. The guy was a contradiction. She had a lot of questions she wanted to ask, but opened it up for him to say his piece first. "You wanted to talk?"

"Those ones you ran into at Jackfish are bad news. Guy's a criminal. You can count on it."

Well, talk about straight to the point. April took her time responding. He must have been watching when she was down there looking for him. He'd seen her with the campers. She wondered how he could tell the guy was a badass. "What makes you so sure?"

"What would you think if I told you they packed up and moved further into the woods after you left?"

"I'd be intrigued." And she was. They had told her they were moving on to Toronto. Why move further into the bush when she hadn't given them any indication she'd be a problem? "They just might want some privacy."

"If I looked like that I'd want some privacy too."

She was as curious about the campers as she was about PH. "What do you know about people's looks?"

She watched the shift in his eyes and could see he was preparing his answer. He seemed calm and calculating. This guy was no idiot. She could tell that question hit closer to home as she watched him smile slightly.

"Let's just say, I've seen some things."

She had to wonder about that. Where? What? And when? She wanted to learn more about this man. "You didn't want to give your name on the phone."

"Look, I'm just trying to do you a favour and let you know about a dangerous situation. It's real. I hope you'll let me go about my business. I assure you I'm not a wanted person or anything. I just want some privacy."

For some strange reason she trusted him. He came forward with seemingly good intentions. Although she wanted to steer the conversation to him and what he was doing at Jackfish, right now she decided to keep it on the campers. She could push for more at a later time. She didn't want to abuse their first meeting. "Okay, well then... thanks for the warning."

"The plate on their truck is 445 733."

She was caught off guard again. Reaching for her notepad she flipped back a few pages. There it was, 445 733. She looked at the wild man and wondered why he had bothered to remember it. It wasn't something most people would think of.

"Can I ask how long you've been down at Jackfish?"

"Since spring time."

"You don't get into town much do you?"

"Not unless I need to."

She still couldn't place it, but something was off. He was giving simple answers on purpose, almost like he was trying to seem unintelligent. Yet she could see the wheels turning behind the eyes. Yes, it was those eyes. It was easy to see why the women in town were all interested.

"How about, where do you come from?" She could tell that was a question too far when he tensed up.

He started to get up. Standing, he gave her an answer, "Let's just say, the big city."

*****

April watched out the window as he climbed into his truck and realized she still had a number of unanswered questions. The one that was bothering her the most as she sat there staring at her notepad was the new number she had written down. 778 245.

Now she hesitated before sending in the request. It was a privacy thing that she knew he wouldn't like, but from her point of view everyone at Jackfish looked like they could be some kind trouble. Until she knew who was who and what she was dealing with, everyone was a concern.

It couldn't hurt to run it and find out. She could leave it at that. As for the campers, well, she was sure if they were criminals their paperwork would be in order, but their plates were going in the system anyway. She typed the request into her laptop and hesitated again one last time before tapping the finger that invaded the wild man's life.

*****

Dragon went into the truck, searching through his bags before jogging off down the trail. He realized things were changing quickly and it was time he had his M99 out. He wanted to run, but kept a level head as he moved steadily down the old road. Then he saw the container.

He was sure that was where the sound had come from. He stopped to check the ground. The tire tracks were fresh. That guy had been here on the property the whole time. Considering there had been no tracks in and out of the container earlier, he assumed the wild man lived around here somewhere, which was a real problem. The guy had probably been watching everything.

He had wanted to keep things simple and not bring trouble down on himself, to do things right and start on a new path in this country. But it was clear that no matter where he went he would have to fight to keep what was his. This secret belonged to him and him alone, and he couldn't allow anyone to get in his way.

He switched into mountain mode, deciding it was time to make himself comfortable. Things were about to get dirty and he wanted to be himself. He started looking around the container for footpaths. When he found one, he knew it had only one place to go, up.

"Hey," he yelled back up the road at his workers. "Come here."

He waited for one of them to make his way down to the container. "I want you to follow this trail to the top of the hill and report back what you find. I will be with the others at the camper."

The Chinese worker nodded and headed up the path.

Dragon was starting to feel a bit better about taking the offensive. He got into the vehicle and pinned the accelerator to the floor as he arm-wrestled the truck and trailer up the washed out road. He didn't stop until he was over the big knoll and away from the container.

"I want this thing back off the trail. You," he pointed, "clear enough brush so I can back it in all the way."

Dragon went back to the truck and got a satellite phone out of his bag. It was the first time he'd needed it. He dialled the only number he had entered into memory.

"Liang?"

"Yes Dragon."

"Things are getting serious down here. I want you to bring me one man who can do a night mission. Be ready for my calls at any time now."

Dragon walked back down the road, past the container and out into the opening. He wouldn't be waiting long. The motel was only a few miles back along the highway. When Liang's car pulled up to drop off the soldier he had questions. "What is happening?"

"People are getting in the way. This is important Liang, I need you to be ready."

Dragon never really answered the question, just sent him back to the motel. He took the soldier and headed back into the woods.

CHAPTER 18

The night was clear. From the top of the hill Phil had a fantastic view of the lake. He wasn't enjoying it though. He clenched the bottle tighter in his trembling hand. He just didn't like Chinese gangs. He couldn't escape the pictures racing through his brain and the sounds echoing in his ears. It was too soon. Too much, too soon.

The images flooded back and he flipped through the scenes like flashing TV screens with every blink of the eye. The forest rang with yelling, laughing, and screaming. The alleyways turned and turned and never ended. He raced in the dark, running out of time.

Fuck off.

Shaking his head from side to side, Phil tried to focus on this current mess instead of past disasters. He had enjoyed his brief visit with April the OPP officer. Talk about good looking, which sure helped, but she was smart and on top of the job. She'd already written their licence plate down. She seemed as concerned about these Chinese travellers as he was. She let him off easy with her questions, but he knew she had a right to know who was hanging around her territory.

It was the Chinese who were stuck in his head. He still wasn't sure if it was a coincidence that they were just passing through, or if they were here for him. He'd seen a vehicle pulling out of the gravel road to Jackfish as he came back from the cop station. He was sure it was a different gangster driving. There were more of them.

It was clear he was on thin ice right now and didn't want to make a mistake. Taking rabbits without a licence was one thing, taking lives was another. He had already made his decision. He wouldn't start anything, but these gangsters had better leave him alone.

He wanted to light up a cigar but his instincts wouldn't let him. That was why he was sitting quietly, tucked inside the tree line surrounding the clearing where he had created his shelter. His normal sitting spot was too exposed. He settled for another shot from the bottle and glanced out at the water as he savoured the feel of the whiskey burning down his throat.

It was late and he ought to call it a night. Looking down at the bottle he realized he'd polished off a good chunk of it. Staring at the whiskey, he was thinking about another drink when he froze. He'd just heard something.

*****

Dragon took aside the soldier Liang dropped off. "This man must not live. You are clear?"

"Yes, I will make sure."

"Good. Do not expect any help from your escort, he is a civilian."

"I understand."

He instructed the worker, who had gone up the trail and found the house earlier in the day, to guide his soldier in the dark. The worker was reluctant until he saw Dragon's hand go to his machete.

"This man is only a hunter with a gun. He will be easy to deal with at night, do whatever needs done," Dragon reminded the soldier.

It took an hour to climb the hill, the worker kept slowing down as branches he couldn't see hit him in the face. The soldier kept pushing him on. The trail was hard to stay on with only dim light to guide them. Once they neared the top it became harder to follow across the exposed rock.

"The house is around here someplace." The worker wasn't sure where to go next.

*****

There it was again, this time he was sure he heard voices and knew they weren't speaking English. He set the bottle down carefully, making sure the glass wasn't going to clink against anything. Silently he slid the safety off his rifle and pointed it in the direction of the voices.

Okay boys.

The sounds were coming from the head of the trail leading up the hill from his container. Looking up at the moon he knew he was in the right spot. It should get a good look at anyone coming into the clearing around the shelter. Then what?

His head cocked to one side, Phil extended his ear towards the sound. There wasn't much sense in looking until something was there. He needed to concentrate on hearing. Then he caught the sound again and snapped his head around.

Hello there.

He could see the silhouettes of two men ducked over and moving quietly. They eased away from the encircling brush onto the open ground surrounding the shelter. Phil waited until they were near the gate to the inner compound.

His eye twitched and he fought to remain calm. He came here to get away from everyone and here they were coming after him. He brought the scope up to his eye and tried to get a better look at the intruders.

He couldn't see much, just the shapes of two men standing there like they were trying to decide what to do next.

Let me help you out.

He played the trigger, sliding his finger back and forth on the steel. It was time. He settled the finger and reminded himself to breathe.

"What the fuck do you guys want?" He didn't know why he was bothering to give them any notice. He wouldn't be able to read their responses. He wanted to see if they froze or jumped. One of them dove out of sight at the unexpected voice, and the other froze.

The rifle bucked against his shoulder as he watched the one frozen in place spin around before falling to the ground. He'd aimed for the arm on purpose. He still wasn't ready to kill, even if the screaming and blood covered walls were invading his brain again.

He was already on his belly, ten feet away from where he had been when the return shots rang out. Someone was shooting back. Well that answered his question, so from his point of view, it was game on. He noted the location of the muzzle flashes in the brush and ignoring the moans of the guy already down, he continued to crawl.

The shooter was inexperienced. He should have moved by now, but the guy kept his position, shooting at the spot he thought Phil was located. Well, his target was now working its way over the side of the hill and along the rocky bank.

Phil inched back up over the top of the hill. He figured he was somewhere behind the shooter. He wanted to blast away in the dark and spray the area where the shooter was hiding. But he also wanted to get up close and personal, because well, it was.

You're mine buddy.

He figured the guy was just off the trail, so he used it to walk quietly up on his prey. A few steps at a time, he inched closer. When the shooter stood up and fired another set of rounds into the brush, Phil had him in his sights, twenty paces ahead.

He set the rifle down and slowly pulled the machete. Then he crept forward until he knew he was in striking distance. Pausing, he calmed himself, then lunged forward. The shooter must have heard him at the last second and turned, bringing his gun to bear.

The blade came down hard on the gun as it went off, the bullet flying past at knee height. His next hard swing was aimed at the hands holding the weapon. He connected with a wrist and the blade went right through, severing it off.

The shooter's scream matched the screaming in Phil's head.

The soldier dropped the rifle. Phil could see the whites of the man's eyes as he stared up in the moonlight. He reached back like he was going to take a swing with a bat and brought the machete around, using the strength of his torso like a whip. The shot was clean to the neck. Even in the dark Phil closed his eyes against the sight of the blade sinking in.

Everything went quiet. Phil had swung downwards with too much angle and the blade had gone through the collarbone and lodged itself into the shoulder. He leaned in and looked at the shooter. Phil could see the tattoos, and he smiled.

"Those tattoos weren't much help."

He put one foot on the shooter for leverage and reefed the blade out of the body. He heard the moans of the first guy he'd winged. Phil retrieved his rifle and carefully worked his way towards the moans with both weapons in hand. He approached the injured man with caution until he was able to stand over him.

Something was off, and he leaned in closer. *Shit.* This guy wasn't a soldier. He looked like one of the workers. Suddenly, the Chinese opened his eyes, registering shock at seeing someone standing above him.

"I'm not a fighter. They made me show them the house on top of the hill."

The guys face was contorted with pain and Phil realized the man was probably an innocent.

Damn it.

Phil got up and went back to the other body. He ripped off a strip of shirt and returned to wrap the worker's arm. When he was sure the bleeding had stopped, he helped the guy up onto his feet.

"Go back down the trail. You need to get to a hospital immediately. You understand?"

The Chinese nodded and bowed a few times as he backed away, obviously happy to be getting out of there alive.

Phil watched him disappear and then sat down right where he was. *What the fuck is happening?* They had come to get him. *How did they find him?*

Here we go again.

*****

Dragon heard the first shot, then the return fire. He listened to the odd gunshot until finally a scream echoed down off the hill. He didn't hear a thing after that. He was getting nervous and realized he was unarmed. Retrieving his rifle from the truck he stepped away from the camper. He didn't need to be a target.

When the sound of someone approaching broke the night, he crouched down and hid in the woods. The injured Chinese's shouts to his comrades made him relax and he stood up.

"Help me, I've been shot."

Dragon watched the other workers come out and help the man. He stepped forward and looked at the arm that they were unwrapping. He had other concerns. "What happened up there?"

"The crazy man was waiting for us in the trees." The man's eyes were the size of plums. He was in shock.

"Where is my soldier?" Dragon leaned in, listening intently.

"He is most surely dead. I heard him scream."

"What makes you think the man is crazy?" Dragon was curious why the worker was in such a state of panic.

"He was carrying a machete and rifle. He was covered in blood and guts. It was on his clothes and all over his face. He didn't even seem to notice, he was blind to it."

Dragon turned to the others. "Is he going to be okay?"

"I need to go to a hospital right now." The worker answered for himself.

That was out of the question. There was no way anyone was leaving. This was getting out of control as it was. "You get help from these men and relax the night. We will decide in the morning when we can see the wound better."

Dragon went to the truck and got out the sat phone again.

"Hello."

"Liang, things have started. You need to position yourself just off the gravel road somewhere so you can watch for anyone coming into Jackfish. I want you to call me if you see anything."

"What has started?" Liang sounded worried.

"Be ready Liang. This is your chance to perform." He clicked off without waiting for a response.

Sitting in the trailer by himself he couldn't stop thinking about Li. He couldn't stop thinking about his discovery either. Still, Li would be invaluable right now. He could hear the workers getting drunk on the bottle he gave them to keep the injured one happy.

He knew he shouldn't have sent a single soldier. It wasn't a lucky number. He reached for his own bottle and knew he should ignore it. He never had liquor in the mountains back home, and was always ready for anything.

*****

The yelling woke Dragon. He jumped out of bed, grabbing his gun and pulling his jacket off the chair by the door. The camper would be a death trap in a firefight. He bolted out the door, diving into the nearby underbrush. Then he realized the yelling was all in Chinese and that the men were scared.

The scream that followed was awful. Then he heard thrashing and noises coming from inside the tree line. "What's going on?" Dragon yelled.

"He went into the woods to piss. Something has happened."

Dragon ran forward. His instincts took over. He preferred to take things head-on. While there was still thrashing he had a chance to surprise. Leaping and crashing through the bush, he could tell by the noise he was close.

Stopping, he tried to focus. When the big shape took form he pulled the trigger. He didn't aim as he fired from the hip, the target was big enough to hit. The animal turned aside at the shot. Whether it was hit or not didn't seem to matter, it jumped backwards and turned into the trees.

Dragon was sure it was a bear. Was that an omen. He didn't know if it was good or bad, but knew which way he was leaning. *What next?* He called the others to drag the dead worker back to camp.

When Dragon realized it was the wounded worker he went from concerned to relieved. That solved one problem. The worker was ripped open around the neck and chest and covered with bloody bite marks. The way his head flopped forward indicated the bear had broken his neck.

Dragon shivered at the thought. As he looked around at the thick forest the trees looked like they were closing in.

CHAPTER 19

Brad Harrison was tucked behind a small table at the bar in Schreiber. The weekend was approaching. He'd been with the railroad for ages, his whole life it seemed. He had most of what he wanted, fishing boats, four-wheelers, and all the hunting equipment he could use. He'd had everything when April was his.

Damned bitch.

In his opinion a woman belonged in her place, which was wherever she needed to be to please her man. He expected supper, sex, and whatever else on demand. Jesus, who did that broad think she was? He liked her in bed. She was a wild one. Maybe that's why he couldn't let it go. That woman was his, whether she saw it or not. He'd wait her out. She was coming back, he was sure.

The bar was in full swing this today as crews came in and out for lunch or a quick beer. A couple tables had been full all afternoon, and a couple were occupied just like his. He reached for his beer. Just thinking about her was pissing him off.

A rough crew came in and gathered at the bar. They had a few shots to go around before starting into the beer. One of the men noticed Brad sitting up against the wall and yelled across the room. "Hey Bradley, hear the wife's banging that wild man down at Jackfish."

The muscles popped on the back of his neck as he flared up. He felt the rush of blood to his brain and flexed his fists. "What'd you say?"

The guy laughed with his buddies. "Easy there son, just hearing that the cruiser's down there a lot lately." He waited a second before getting his dig in. "And she's a hot one, so you can't blame the guy."

Brad's chair crashed backwards to the floor. He stormed around the table towards the bar. There was an edge to the men's laughter as they began to back away from the loudmouth who was giving Brad the gears.

Brad knew the CP boys were tough, he was one of them. But this guy had just given him something he'd been looking for all day, an excuse to let go. He'd give the loudmouth credit, he was playing the tough guy part well, the question was how far was he willing to go. Because Brad was going all the way on this one.

"You want to say something about her again?"

The loudmouth looked at his buddies who had moved slightly away and smiled, he turned back to Brad. "Hey there buddy, back off. She's single because you blew your shot. Now hopefully I'll get a chance at her."

A kick from the steel toed work boot did most of the damage, giving Brad the upper hand. The blow landed right below his opponent's knee and the railroader buckled. As the man's head fell forward, Brad met it with a rising knee, the blow knocking the guy over backwards. He landed with a crack as his head bounced off the floor.

Brad stepped forward to finish the job. He could almost see his foot ramming into the soft stomach. Motion from the side slowed him down as the other railroaders moved in to protect their buddy. "All right, that's enough." They got between Brad and the downed man, pushing him back.

He took a second to calm down and come back from some crazy place. The guy was lucky he wasn't dead. Jesus, he was pissed. He threw himself back down into a chair at the table, aware everyone was watching him. *Well fuck them.*

He drank hard from his glass of beer and thought about what they had said. She was seeing some guy at Jackfish. Who the hell lived there? He knew he was going to lose it, so he downed a few more beers while he worked himself into a rage.

*****

April had been preoccupied all day. She wasn't even responding to the radar when it went off. Instead, she flashed her cherries for a second and watched each speeding vehicle's front end drop like a rock as the drivers hit the brakes.

She was thinking about the reports that had been waiting on her desk when she came in that morning. She actually had a request to call back on the camper plates. She phoned the Vancouver RCMP detachment which left the call back request and got talking to a Sergeant with his own set of questions.

"You have an interest in a vehicle from out our way?"

"Yup, bad looking guys, tattoos and all."

"That figures. We traced the truck and camper to a holding company. It's one we associate with triad business."

"Okay, so what now?"

"Not much, unless they're doing something illegal. Where are they?"

"I'm not sure if they're still in the area or not. They said they were going to Toronto."

"Makes sense, those guys are strongest in Montreal, Toronto, and Vancouver."

"Well, it's good to know the situation, even if they're gone. Thanks."

"If they're still around you're best to keep an eye on them. These are seriously bad people."

She kept thinking back to her encounter with the gangsters, she was probably lucky, something could have happened if she'd pushed any further. Especially with the one who had stayed sitting in the background. It was obvious the talker was the leader, he'd been pretty confident for a young guy. The question was, were they still down there?

She thought about going for lunch in Schreiber, the weekend was finally here and that usually brought some kind of trouble. Then she thought better of it and took a few bites off the apple she had thrown in her glove box. It never hurt to have something with her.

Did she really want a second confrontation? If they were moving on and didn't cause a problem, why get involved? She wasn't a hard-ass and would rather avoid a dust-up when she could. Still, there was something about those guys that spelled trouble and even if it didn't come her way, it was still going to come at someone else, somewhere down the line.

That was one of the problems she had with the job. You needed evidence. A crime had to be committed before she could do anything. Stuff like that drove her nuts. The cops knew who was a problem and who wasn't. Which locals were criminals and who weren't. She couldn't just go in and shut them down, put people in jail and be done with it. They had rights apparently and deserved proper procedure, which made no sense when the criminals never followed the rules themselves.

Why her two issues had to be mixed was really what was getting at her as she sat on the side of the highway. If it was just the campers, knowing they were supposed to be heading out, she would probably just let them go. But it was the information from the second set of licence plates that was really bothering her.

She'd been shocked when she had received the report back on the wild man. She had found herself sitting at her desk just staring at it. Then found herself rereading it. Somehow that made some things fall into place. Like his level of concern about the Chinese. But it threw pretty well everything else into a state of confusion.

What had happened to the guy? Why was he living in the woods? And what did he look like under that hair and beard. *She didn't just think that did she? Jesus.* Although she did have to admit her curiosity was becoming more personal. Their brief visit confirmed that the women around town were on to something.

Now she was downright intrigued. She just had to understand the contrast between past and present. She wasn't as concerned now from a professional point of view. He surely couldn't be a threat could he?

It was the fact that both he and the Chinese were down at Jackfish that was drawing her like a magnet. She kept checking her watch, as if another passing half hour made any difference. She just couldn't get it off her mind. She never would have guessed.

Late in the afternoon the cruiser pulled off the highway and turned down the gravel road to the Jackfish siding. April had given in to her urge to be proactive. Now she had the shotgun on the seat beside her and the clasp on her side arm open as the SUV crept slowly down the road.

Approaching the clearing she could see the campers were gone, which gave her some sense of relief. She stopped and got out at the spot anyway and looked around. She followed the tire marks and couldn't see where they turned around. Instead they seemed to head further into the clearing, along the railroad tracks.

She kept following them until she realized the marks continued along towards the hill and rock cut at the end. She decided she might as well get the truck.

*****

Phil heard the vehicle coming down the gravel road and wondered if the gangsters were getting reinforcements. He didn't care, he was ready for them. He'd stayed on guard all night with just the bottle for company. A few times he'd swung the rifle around madly at imagined sounds. The trees kept changing to alleyways and the wind became an endless screaming echoing in his ears.

He squinted as the sun came up, taking a moment to enjoy the warmth. It seemed to push back his memories. No one else had bothered him during the night, but he had been ready for anything.

When he saw the black and white he wasn't sure if he felt relief, or dread.

"Now what?"

He knew he had to deal with it, and at least she had seen him before. Phil got up and started jogging down the hill. This wasn't going to go well.

*****

April drove along the siding. She had a good view of the tire tracks she thought were from the camper. When they turned towards the trail at the back of the mountain, she hesitated. Were they in there, and did they hear her coming?

She put the cruiser in park and grabbed the shotgun. Looking the gun over one last time, she made sure it was loaded and ready to use. Standing there for a moment, she let herself get dialled in. The thick forest, shifting shadows, and wind in the trees were all distractions. She needed to be careful.

She was about to step onto the old road when she noticed movement to her left. She aimed the barrel of her shotgun and waited. There it was, a blur through the trees, then a shape coming down towards the container. She decided to wait for whoever it was out in the open.

She watched the figure materialize into the camouflaged wild man. She felt herself start to relax, but the feeling was momentary. *My God.* She shivered once, the vibration running from her feet, right up through her spine.

He looked wilder than before. Christ, he looked like a madman and he reeked of alcohol. What was that all over him? *Shit.* April felt her stomach sink. *Shit.* Blood was everywhere. The machete hanging from his waist even had dried blood on the handle. He held a rifle loosely in his right hand.

Something very bad had happened here. *Fuck.* She took a step backwards and looked him in the eye. He was staring at her with a look of sadness. It didn't match his body language, which was saying psycho.

"What the hell is going on? What have you done?" She didn't wait for him to answer. "What's happened to you? You're a retired cop for Christ's sake."

When he finally spoke, she really wished he hadn't.

"It's worse than that." Phil looked back over his shoulder. "I killed a guy last night. His body is up on the hill."

All of April's training kicked in. She raised her shotgun and started yelling. "Freeze right there. Drop the rifle and raise your hands."

He hesitated.

"Right fucking now!"

Book 3
Resolve

CHAPTER 20

April Harrison stood there staring down the wild man who she was now sure was Phil Hardy.

"Phil, last chance. Put it down."

He seemed to respond to his name and slowly leaned forward to place the rifle on the ground. Stepping back he raised his hands, not up in the air, but out to the side.

She thought about the machete but figured she had him covered now. *Okay, what next?* Dead bodies were not the norm around here and she was trying hard to sort out procedures from adrenaline driven urges. "Okay, you need to be straight now Phil. You are Phil Hardy?"

"Yes."

"Retired cop from Toronto?"

"Yes."

She knew there had to be a lot more to it. First, he was too young to be retired, that usually meant he'd given it up. The question was why. Second, his records were sealed, which was unusual. She should have been able to get a history. It was supposed to be open information, but for some reason his files were coming up restricted.

"Who's dead?"

"Chinese gangster."

She didn't want to hear that, although to be honest it was better than a local. "What happened?"

"I had a bad feeling about those guys, and hid out in the woods instead of going back to the shelter. Then two of them showed up in the dark sneaking around the fence." He shrugged his shoulders. "I gave them a chance to explain and they went to ground. I wasn't waiting for them to come get me."

She put herself in his shoes. Dark, late at night, no one should have been up there at all and Phil was probably lucky he'd been on guard. Now she had to decide if she believed his story. She had to figure out if he was under attack, or in some way involved in whatever this was.

Was he innocent and deserving of some protection? Or should she run him down to the station?

"So there's two of them up there?"

"No, just one."

"Where's the other one?

"I shot him in the arm, then realized he wasn't a soldier. So I wrapped him up to stop the bleeding and let him go."

"Go where?"

"I'm assuming to the camper with those other gangsters."

Christ, this was getting intense. She could have gangsters in the woods. She did have a killer right in front of her. He stood there so damn calmly that it was irritating. "You've shot people before haven't you?"

She watched him force a smile.

"Let's just say, I've had to."

There was that answer again. *Let's just say.* Did he mean he was giving her a line, or was it that he was implying he couldn't say?

She needed to get a look at the dead body, then the wounded man. She studied Phil, trying to gauge him. She wanted to believe him, but it was hard under the circumstances. She realized she'd been squeezing the shotgun so hard her forearms hurt. Slowly she loosened her fingers.

"I can trust you, right?"

"You can trust I'll do the right thing."

She wasn't sure if that was the answer she wanted, but decided to move forward. "Okay show me the body."

His arm moved. "Can I bring my rifle?"

She could see his concern and realized the problem was still out there. She had to keep an eye on the ex-cop but she had better be ready for anything from the Chinese. She nodded and then let him lead her up the trail behind the container.

As Phil stepped out into the clearing, he stopped and waited while she caught up. Oh God. She wanted to look away, but needed to focus and do her job. The man lay sprawled in the dirt like a rag doll. His left arm looked awkward without its hand, but it was the dismembered head hanging to one side that made her stomach churn. *Jesus.* She was a traffic cop.

Then she realized that this Chinese was not one of the men she had seen earlier at the camper. "This isn't one of the campers."

"I know, and that's what concerns me. There are more of them."

She dug out her notepad and started scribbling furiously, trying to regain her composure. She didn't look at the body again. There was no use, it wouldn't help. So there were even more gangsters running around than they knew about. That wasn't going to help. What was going on here?

She needed a diversion, time to think. "So you live up here?"

"Yes, up this way." He headed towards a clearing on top of the hill.

She let him get a bit ahead, trying to regain her composure and not wanting to be caught off guard by anything. But then she caught sight of his shelter. She found herself staring at the enclosure. Metal posts and wire fencing surrounded the exposed top of the hill. Not even a bear was getting in there.

The shelter itself was interesting, the large canvas dome with a big semi-circular plastic window section faced out over the lake. The wooden platform Phil had anchored the structure to, formed a deck running around the dome. On one hand it looked insufficient, but then on the other it looked adventurous. She really was surprised by it. She noticed that Phil had turned at the front of the shelter and headed towards the cliff edge. She followed behind him, stopping just short of where he was standing.

What a sight. You could see the lake in almost every direction. The trains would pass through the rock cut right below. Noticing the makeshift bench she realized he sat out here and stared out over Superior. She could relate, her eyes were drawn to the water like magnets. It sure looked peaceful.

Jesus woman, get your shit together. She shook herself. There was nothing peaceful here right now. She wasn't processing things right and she was making mistakes. She knew she should have called in backup, or at the very least, registered her position. She left him standing there and went over to the cliff looking east, down over the rail siding.

She could see he had a great view there as well. He would have seen her and the campers on the other side of the clearing, it was apparent now that the reflections she'd seen had been him watching. She bent out over the edge to look down at a steeper angle and caught a glimpse of the cruiser. Good.

She hadn't realized that he'd followed her, turning she almost ran into him. She jumped back then remembered the cliff. His face became alarmed.

"Easy there." He backed away to give her room.

April moved away from the ledge and let her breath out. She needed to get some control over herself. "Where are the Chinese parked now?"

"They went up the old road a bit and then pushed the camper into the trees."

"You've seen it?"

"Yeah, I confronted them and they said they were moving on shortly."

"You don't look like you believe that."

"Does it matter now?"

April realized it didn't. She had to make a call. The option to arrest the ex-cop and take him in still existed, but it was starting to look like he had just been caught up in something beyond his control. She thought he could argue self-defence. Somewhere inside her head she also knew that the body on the trail had been through too much.

Something about Phil was a little off, but deep down he seemed to be on the right side.

Now she was left with an injured guy who had a bunch of gangsters keeping him company. Should she check it out, or get backup?

*****

Phil watched her. She was working the scene, processing all the details. He would be too in her shoes. He could tell she was still unsure about him, but the fact he was still carrying his gun was a good sign. He knew he would need it again. It was just a matter of time.

He was trying to keep her relaxed, but his own emotions were still firing and he was busy with his own thoughts. He should have finished it all last night. Now she was here and he had to be careful.

"Could have been over by now."

"Did you say something?"

He had said it out loud, too used to living alone. "No just talking to myself."

"Living up here, you'll be doing a lot more of it."

He looked over and saw she was kidding. "Hey, it's only a problem if I hear another voice talking back." He caught her brief smile. "We need to go and check out these campers. The sooner the better."

She looked shocked.

"I'll help you and show you where they are." He could tell she hadn't got herself to that point yet. "You can't ignore these guys now."

"I know that!"

He sensed she was rattled and decided to take a different tack. "Look, let me get you some water or something and you can take a second to sort it out." He could see her relief at the new option and he pointed towards the dome. "It isn't much but I call it home."

*****

April stopped by the fence and watched him open the gate latches. Climbing up on the deck she took in the view. *Unbelievable.* The door was a simple flap system and she slipped through into the interior.

Wow. Inside a web of triangle shaped tubes fitted together to make the dome. She looked up and spotted a clear plastic opening that looked to the sky. Small clear circles lower down acted like windows. The whole thing was much bigger than it looked from outside.

The plastic semi-circular window in the front was taller than she was. Standing for a moment she stared out over the water. Turning to look around the inside, she spotted a bed perched on a raised platform at the back. She could picture laying there and either looking up at the stars or watching the waves on the lake.

A small table with a propane stove seemed to double as a kitchen off to one side, and she hoped there was a washroom behind that freestanding wall. Did he have water here? She could tell the wood stove wasn't in use yet, she wondered if it could heat this thing. Winters got pretty cold around here. The place really was amazing.

He folded himself down beside a small knee-high table. April realized he meant for her to sit as well and lowered herself to a small cushion on the floor. For some reason it seemed more intimate than sitting on chairs.

"So why you here Phil?"

He hesitated, as if he was thinking about how to answer.

"I fucked up, lost it. I needed to get away."

She knew it wasn't the right time to get into details, but was still concerned, would he lose it again? Fuck up again? What had he done?

"You did something wrong?" Might as well find out now.

"Yeah, I killed a bunch of gangsters."

Well, he wasn't getting any better at stopping that from happening was he? "It seems like they keep finding you."

His eyes snapped towards her, looking at her like she knew something he didn't. All she'd said was that they were coming to him. Was that it? Was he expecting them?

"You don't know any of these guys do you?" She suddenly had doubts.

"Absolutely not."

She had to accept that and switched to thinking about checking out the campers. "I think we'll go down to the truck and make a call, then go in on foot and look for those campers."

"No, we can't do that," Phil shook his head.

She looked at him, waiting for an explanation.

"If we go down there they will be watching the road. It's just not the smartest way. I have a trail along the top of the hills."

He wanted her to walk in the opposite direction of her cruiser, which was hard to do, but his reasoning was sound. They probably would be watching the road.

April agreed reluctantly. "All right, let's go."

*****

Phil was pleased with her decision, he wanted at them again. He was sure they were here for him and he was worried the past had come back again. Where did he have to go to get away from it? His professional exterior was hiding what he felt as he smiled.

The stack of milk crates serving as a nightstand held his ammo. He grabbed a handful of shells and loaded his pockets. He was doing as much damage as he could if he got the chance. He saw her watching him. She probably wanted to say something, but needing his help she held her tongue.

"Right call there sweetie."

"You talking to yourself again?"

He looked over and realised what he'd said. "Yup. But I'm ready to go."

She seemed to take a last look around before heading towards the door. He had to admire her a bit. She didn't seem scared or the slightest bit hesitant. Yet they both knew anything could happen.

*****

Dragon was fighting with himself, he wanted to just walk up the hill and get it over with. He also knew he had to live to enjoy his discovery. He wasn't used to sending others into battle in his place. Except Li, and he was gone.

The sat phone rang and Dragon knew they had company. "What's up Liang?"

"A cop truck has driven down to the siding."

This wasn't good. Did the police know about the shooting last night? He could see the potential for things to unravel now. Trouble kept finding him. He needed to think, but time wasn't on his side. As he made the decision in his head he knew it was a big one.

"Disable the dammed cop truck and find me on the old road behind the hill."

"A cop truck? This can't be the way."

"Liang, I thought you knew not to question or to think. Aren't you a triad soldier?"

"Yes, but…"

"There are no 'buts' Liang. Do it quick."

"What do you want me to do?"

Dragon liked the question, it meant Liang was past the not doing it and on to the how. "Try to hide the fact it was a cop truck." He hung up and left Liang to sort it out. He had other things to worry about. How long had the cops been here and where were they? How many of them were there and was the wild man with them?

Dragon knew he was losing his hold on the workers. The three remaining men were still in shock over their comrade getting shot and then attacked by the bear. Dragon hadn't told them to do anything yet, so they just stood around. That worked. He'd use them as distractions.

He eased into the bush behind the camper carrying his rifle. When he was sure no one had seen him leave and he was in an area of dense brush, he sat down. For the first time he felt like he used to in the mountains back home. He was taking the initiative.

CHAPTER 21

Liang's vehicle crawled down the gravel road, stopping at the entrance to the clearing. He could see the cruiser on the other side of the open area, near the hill. He let one soldier out to watch the road while he and the other two drove towards the black and white.

He was in too deep now. Once you start taking it to the cops you bring shit down on your head. He considered leaving Dragon and his mission. There was nothing stopping him from turning around and driving until he hit Vancouver.

But if Dragon ever made it back and the bosses found out he had abandoned the man, then he would pay a price. The question he had to wrestle with was where would the price be highest, the cops, or his bosses.

He was supposed to make it hard to identify the vehicle. Luckily, it had no roof-mounted lights, just the ones inside the cab. He would have had to rip off the outside lights or they would have stood out no matter what he did.

"We blow it. Open the gas lid and run something inside to set on fire."

The soldiers made a long wick of torn cloth, inserting it deep into the gas filler. Liang checked the doors. To his surprise they were open. He took some of the loose papers in the truck and made a pile under the front seat.

When he was sure that the others were ready with the gas tank, he started the pile burning, leaving the driver's door wide open. Nodding to his men, they lit the material hanging from the side of the cruiser.

Liang was shaking. There was no turning back now. He got his soldiers in the car and they back-peddled to the gravel road where he had left the man watching. From this point he could watch the truck burn without being too close.

Even from across the clearing they could see the flames licking up the side of the truck and shooting out the door of the cab. He was glad they were in the middle of nowhere because the noise was going to be loud when it blew. The worst thing was, he didn't know why they were here in the first place, or what he was actually involved in.

All he could do was let it burn and then go find Dragon.

*****

Dragon sensed the movement before he saw it. He was in the zone now. Sitting in the woods listening to the wind in the branches had brought his mind and body together. Now he strained to hear what he knew was trouble coming his way.

The workers were still hanging around the camp, he could hear them every once in a while. He took the hundredth look at his rifle, making sure it was ready. There it was again. Just a few branches moving, but the noise sounded louder than he expected, moving more than the wind could move them.

He stared in the direction of the sound, but didn't focus on anything in particular, waiting for his peripheral vision to pick up whatever it was. Then there was nothing. He knew whoever it was had stopped because they were close to the camp. He brought the gun up and waited.

"Damned trees." He couldn't see much through the branches and waited for his opponents to take their next step. Shit, they were above him on the hill. He was in a bad position, they had the better angle. He was sure there were two of them just by the sounds they made. Keeping the gun close to his cheek, his eyes scanned the forest, but he kept the scope close in case he needed it. Then he got his chance when he heard the voice. Was he too exposed to take it?

A woman's voice yelled out, breaking the quiet. "Everyone freeze! This is the police."

The workers were stunned, two just stood there, while the third started to run. Dragon heard a rifle shot just as he raised the scope to his eye. Now he had her in his sights.

*****

April followed Phil along the hilltop trail and through the brush as he turned down towards the old road. He explained that they should be near the camper. She let him lead, creeping along behind him, while he took his time sneaking down the hill.

He stopped and motioned her up beside him before he pointed through the trees. "There it is, see the blue and white?"

"Yeah, okay."

April moved in front of him and continued the descent step by step. She was cautious and wanted to make sure she had the advantage. She could make out shapes by the camp and could tell there were people moving around. She knew there was no good way to go about it, and since she already had one body, she wasn't giving anyone the benefit of the doubt.

"Everyone freeze, this is the police."

The gunshot, so close, scared the hell out of her. She'd been focused on the camper and hadn't expected Phil to open up. *Christ.* She watched the worker who tried to run thrown down awkwardly. Then the muzzle flash from the woods near the trailer caught her attention. The tree in front of her exploded into bits of bark flying in every direction.

She heard Phil's second shot as she hit the ground, but wasn't sure where he was aiming. This was more than she'd expected. She really needed backup. Before April could react an explosion rocked the forest.

The thunderous bang was shocking and she slammed her hands down, grabbing the forest floor to keep her balance. Everyone in the woods looked down the old road towards the clearing but couldn't see anything. The explosion had been like a vacuum, sucking the air right out of the forest.

The next couple of minutes were filled with an eerie silence. April couldn't figure it out until she felt the hand on her shoulder. She looked back at Phil and his mouth was moving. She was shocked she couldn't hear him and took a second to close her eyes and centre herself. "Get it together April."

"What?"

She realized he was listening. "Never mind let's get out of here." She shook her head to clear it. She could see from the stone-cold expression on his face he was on autopilot. "Phil! Let's go."

His eyes finally focused on her and he nodded. Good, she had his attention. She started to move, keeping low as they retraced their route up the hill. She was surprised that there weren't any more shots fired. Phil moved quickly and she pushed to keep up.

At the top of the hill he slowed and waited for her. Once out of the woods she could see his face better, the snarl that curled the corner of his lip said he was into it. Well she wasn't.

April took off running along the exposed trail, wanting to get away from that spot as quickly as possible. She heard his pounding feet running behind her. There was a bad feeling in her gut as she ran past the shelter towards the cliff.

She stopped and looked over the side of the hill towards the clearing below.

"Oh no."

*****

Phil was running behind her. He was trying to think as he went. The gangsters had been ready for them, expecting them. It all pointed to bad news. He had taken a shot at the guy who ran, assuming if he running he was guilty, sure that anyone he put down wasn't going to be shooting back.

When he saw the muzzle flash in the bush and branches exploding in front of April he shifted gears, swinging his rifle, getting another shot off. They couldn't stay there. The shooter knew where they were, exposed against the hillside. He'd seen her confusion when he grabbed her shoulder but she reacted quickly and they were moving.

The explosion had caught him off guard and he couldn't figure out what it was. He should never have used the same trail as the other day. It had almost got her killed. When she ran past the shelter towards the cliff, his mind jumped to the cruiser. "Oh, shit."

He stopped beside her, looking down. The fire was burning out. Flames were still flickering but the wreck was mostly smoldering, the smoke blowing away in the slight breeze.

"Well that's interesting." The strange look she gave him said she didn't find it too interesting at all.

Something moved at the end of the siding, he was sure of it. He raised the scope and scanned the other side of the clearing. There was a guy standing beside the gravel road. Phil laid on the ledge and set the rifle down in front of him. Stretched out, he took his time, leaning on his arms. He brought the scope to his eye. The tattoos were all he needed to see.

It was a long shot and the wind would have an effect. He knew his rifle and figured out the angles. He moved the crosshair a notch up and two over from the target. Back in his granddad's day the thirty-ought-six Winchester had been a topnotch sniper rifle. Nowadays folks around here carried them because you could drop a full-grown moose or a charging bear with a single heavy-grain round. He was going to take a shot and then move a notch back towards centre and get off a second.

He took one last flex of his fingers before settling on the trigger. Taking a breath, he let it out. His finger squeezed slightly and the rifle jerked. He moved the sight one notch back and touched the trigger again. The gun jumped one more time and he let the smoke drift away from the barrel. Raising his head away from the scope, he blinked a few times.

"You got him with the first one."

Phil felt the effects of the day catching up to him. It took some effort to scramble up off the ground. He looked at her and didn't know what to say. The adrenaline was wearing off and he wanted to sit down for a minute. He fought to keep his hands from shaking. He didn't want her to see. What he really needed was some sleep.

He looked up to gauge the time and knew the day was done, darkness would be moving in shortly. "You can stay here the night, it's getting too dark to walk out of here. It might not be safe."

"There was only one shooter at the camper, so we should be able to move."

"No. While he was shooting, someone else was doing the cruiser. We don't know how many are out there at all. Get some rest and water. Take a break, let's rethink this."

He didn't wait for an answer and headed towards the enclosure.

Once she was settled and he knew she was okay, he excused himself. "I've got a few things to take care of. I'll be back shortly."

He knew she wanted to protest by the way her lips moved a few times. He didn't have much time and left her to her confusion.

It had seemed ridiculous at the time when he had partially set these simple traps. When he left the city he thought someone might come looking. He hadn't hooked them up completely, in case some innocent person came along. Now he needed them set and ready.

There was nothing else he could do except wait. He took a last look around and headed back to the shelter.

CHAPTER 22

Dragon dropped down into the brush, moving low and quick, ten yards to the left. As he moved he could hear the couple retreating back up the hill and knew his opportunity was gone. There were just too many trees.

He didn't take any chances when he heard the vehicle coming up the trail, even though it should be Liang. There was a sense of relief when the car stopped and he watched his soldiers get out. Now he had some tools.

Stepping out of the brush he nodded at Liang and noticed the man looked scared. He could see the concern in his eyes and his body was tense. Dragon didn't have time for it. "The cruiser?"

"Taken care of."

"Okay." Dragon was committed now. He really wanted to get to his find, but this dangerous interruption could upend everything. He needed to clear the hill and make the place go quiet. He looked at the two men with Liang and wondered if they were up to the task. They'd better be.

"Get out all your weapons and make sure you're ready to go."

"What are we doing?"

"Don't worry Liang, just get ready while we wait for dark."

Dragon watched the men getting out their bags while his thoughts switched to the couple on top of the hill. The woman wasn't an issue. She wasn't a warrior, that much had been evident earlier in the day.

Even though she was carrying a gun she hadn't used it, instead falling to the ground in confusion. It was the wild man who had killed the running worker, and he was the one who had returned fire to protect her. The cop didn't seem to have any experience so she could be a coin flip. Might fight well, but he was betting she might also fold.

The wild man was a whole other thing. Dragon had known the first time he saw him that he was serious trouble and had been in the thick of things once or twice. Now that the man had shown his hand Dragon knew the guy was on his game, ready and willing. He had his first doubts about sending in the soldiers, wondering if it was a waste of men.

*****

It was getting dark on the hill and Phil and April fidgeted, taking turns looking out the large window. Sitting in the dome didn't seem safe the darker it got. April's brain worked on two different issues at the same time. The first was Phil and his dome. She kept trying to imagine what drove him to live in this way.

She looked around at the simplicity of the place. The openness gave it a sense of freedom that tied it to the wilderness. He seemed at peace here and she tried to imagine him working the concrete streets of the city. She couldn't, at least not now. She'd been intrigued by his past, but had spent the better part of the last two hours talking about herself. He was either a good listener or else a good interrogator.

"We're not staying in here are we?"

"Nope. Get some more coffee into you."

Twenty minutes later he was up and rummaging through a crate in the corner. "Okay, we better get out of here. Here's a coat that will hide those reflective stripes on your jacket."

April took it, it wouldn't cover her legs, but it was better than nothing. She started preparing mentally.

The second thing that she had been thinking about was the Chinese. This situation had gone past the point of talking, or trying to apprehend. They had shot at her, even when she had announced herself. Now up here in the dark there was no doubt she'd be shooting first and asking questions later. God, this whole thing was going to hell.

She followed Phil outside the enclosure towards the cliff. He turned to her. "We'll stay against the cliff. No one can come up behind us."

The logic made sense.

"You can get down here by these rocks." He pointed her to a sheltered spot where two fractured granite slabs came together and then he crouched behind another boulder near the edge. "I'll be behind this one and we should be able to keep an eye on each other."

Again, she couldn't see anything wrong with the setup. "Seems good to me." Although what was the proper setup for this type of shootout? Was there one?

"Don't wander away from here. I have traps out there and I don't want you caught in them," he warned.

What? April was still not clear about Phil in her head. He had traps out there? For what? Jesus, the man just might be crazy after all. She didn't know what to say. "Okay."

"If I get up and leave my position don't worry, I'll be back."

Great, take off and leave me with the traps. This was getting more out of hand every minute. But then it had been out of hand ever since the truck blew up. She would do her part. "I'm ready, let's just wait them out."

He seemed to like her answer, nodded, and settled down behind his boulder. Now was the waiting, she focused on the edge of the forest letting her eyes settle into a soft stare. She was tired but the adrenalin was keeping her alert.

*****

The three men moved single file up the trail from the storage container. With sharp ledges and sheer rock walls covered in brush and trees, there was no thought of bushwhacking and making their own trail. It would make too much noise and who knew where they would end up in the dark.

Liang kept the two soldiers in front of him, shining a flashlight past them as they walked. It made better sense to have the light out in front, but he was staying in the back and so was the light. He was doing the job, but the story about the wild man on the hill had his nerves on edge.

Dragon had said the guy wasn't a problem. It was just that he had a gun and could shoot. That sure sounded like a problem to Liang. He'd beat people up and disposed of a few bodies for his bosses, but he'd never deliberately gone out to kill someone. And Dragon had made that point clear. Absolutely no one was to survive. Liang had one more thought. *Major important that I survive.*

The going was slow and his men were worried about every branch and twig that moved. He was going to kill a cop, shit he didn't want to, but he didn't feel he had a choice.

Half an hour up the hill, they were working their way around a rock face when the beam from his flashlight caught something. A rope? He realized the first soldier had stepped over it by luck, but the second one had his foot snagged in it.

Quickly Liang jumped forward and pushed the man. He kept pushing as he heard the crash of falling rocks. With a last effort he lunged forward, landing beside the soldier who fell to his hands and knees.

The falling rocks barely missed them as they tumbled onto the trail. The last boulder to bounce over the edge was as big as a man and would have crushed them if they hadn't been so quick. He knew they were safe, but what the hell was that? A trap?

The fear was beginning to eat at him. He was used to bars, alleys, and other people's fear. This was a whole new ball game. Liang took a couple quick breaths and focused his eyes more. He knew now that they were playing for real.

When they came to a large tree trunk partially blocking the trail, with branches that acted like a fence, Liang took charge. "Wait a minute."

He flashed the light up and down over the obstruction. He couldn't see any rope or trap. The forest was too thick on either side of the trail to go around the wall of branches, so they grabbed a handful each and started to pull the tree out of the way.

Suddenly there was movement from the side and above them. A few smaller side trees folded in and a large tree fell directly out of the sky towards the trail. Liang and one of the soldiers jumped backwards, but the third one tried to jump forward and caught his foot on a root. He panicked, falling forward while trying to rip his foot out.

The large trunk slammed down pinning the soldier to the ground, breaking his back and hips in the process. He screamed and Liang rushed to quiet him. The guy was about to pass out from the pain and couldn't stop himself. Liang reached back and drove him in the side of the head, knocking him out cold. He couldn't have anyone zeroing in on the noise. Looking down at the contorted body he knew the guy was done anyways.

Now Liang was scared to stay still or to move forward. He knew he needed to make it to the top and get off the damned trail.

*****

Phil was starting to tire. He kept looking across to see if April was okay. She wasn't moving much, but he could make out her outline against the dark stone. He had liked watching her relaxed and enjoying his shelter and he realized he'd been missing something.

"Wake up man."

He leaned his head back and held it there, his neck muscles were sore. Then he heard the falling rocks. He knew where they were. That was the first trap. It was a series of larger and larger rocks that he found piled precariously against each other just above the trail. He'd tied a rope to a small rock that acted like a keystone at the bottom holding it all together. Then he'd stretched the rope across the trail hoping that a pull on the rope would be enough to bring the whole thing down.

Phil wondered how many of them there were and if he had snagged one. Well, what he meant was, had he crushed one. A quick look over at April and he knew they were still doing fine. The next trap was near the first one, and he listened. The large pine had fallen over and become hung up on some smaller birches and was now stuck hanging above the trail. He'd used his machete to chop at the trees on the sides until they were held only by a sliver of bark. As soon as someone tried to pull out the tree he'd placed on the trail, wedged into the birches, the whole thing would crash down.

The scream broke the night stillness wide open. Well he'd gotten at least one there. The shrieks suddenly stopped. It didn't look good for whoever it was. Phil knew their enemies were close now. He balanced his rifle on the rock, training it on the opening in the tree line. If they came through there that was their mistake.

Minutes passed before a figure stepped abruptly into the clearing. Phil's finger was twitching on the trigger. He wanted to hurt.

His brain kept flipping back and forth into the past.

He was racing against the clock, knowing the deadline had elapsed. He ran through the endless alleyways. Twisting, turning, running. Hearing nothing but the sound of his feet pounding against the pavement. Another alley, and then another. He knew their lives depended on him. Someone stepped out in front of him as he ran and he raised one of his gun hands and shot them point-blank. Another tried to grab him. He kicked out, not wasting a bullet. He was running. Running. The sound of his own labored breathing roaring in his ears...

Phil snapped back to the present and picked up a silhouette in his rifle sight. The figure was ten to fifteen feet into the opening. He knew that April should be able to see the guy by now. Something made him hold off. He wanted to make sure there weren't any others. Then he saw movement.

"Bingo."

He watched the second figure, bent over and moving step by step, cautiously.

"Smarter, eh?"

This was a thinker. Hopefully it was the boss. Phil didn't waste time and looked through the scope, he'd see better with it, even in the dark. The guy was making it easy with his slow deliberate movements and Phil was sure he had him. The crack of his rifle broke the silence. The thinker went down, but Phil wasn't sure. Then the night exploded.

The first figure, who Phil had ignored, swung around and opened up in his direction. At the same time April let go with her shotgun. Its loud boom echoed off the hills. The guy didn't fire again, but Phil could hear rustling in the underbrush as someone hightailed it. They could follow his progress as he stumbled and crashed down the steep side of the hill.

"You okay?" He called out.

"Yeah, I'm good."

"Stay put."

They stayed that way for an hour to make sure there was no one else coming up the hill. Finally Phil stood and walked around the rock. "Let's take a break. We should be good until they regroup."

He stepped over to where the body should be, his rifle held ready, just in case. He shook his head as he looked down at the dead man. This wasn't one of the campers either. *Damn. How many were there?*

He could tell April was shook up and the thought of a second go-around wasn't that appealing to her.

"Get ready honey, cause they'll be back," he said to himself as he looked at the woods.

*****

Outside the camper Dragon sat up straight, clenched fists gripping the arms of his chair as the crashing rocks broke the silence. He was listening intently when a scream echoed off the hill. His men must be at the top. The ensuing quiet seemed to last forever and then there was a single shot followed by an explosive barrage from different guns.

The next period of silence was maddening. He wanted to know what was happening. Did Liang do his job? Another five minutes passed before he heard the crashing in the woods. Someone was coming straight down the hill, no matter the obstacles. Dragon raised his rifle.

The soldier smashed his way through the last trees and stumbled onto the old road. Orienting himself, he started towards the trailer. Dragon jumped up to meet him. "What happened? Where's Liang?"

"I don't know where he is. There were ambushes and shotguns up there." He pointed to his arm and leg mangled by buckshot. "I've been hit."

"How many were there? Where were they?"

"They were waiting for us. They had traps and then started shooting from somewhere. I shot back and was hit. I don't know how many there were."

Dragon was pissed. He wanted to shoot this guy right here. "You came back? Why didn't you continue to fight?"

"I didn't know the land up there. You can fall off the edge. I had to get out of there. It was an ambush."

If he had more soldiers he would have shot this one right now. But he might need him yet. He felt his anger building. It really was time for this to end. He should have done it himself, that had always been the way.

He looked up at the hill in the darkness. Enjoy the quiet up there for now. It's me you're dealing with next.

CHAPTER 23

Brad Harrison was drunk and ready to sort things out. He believed that if you wanted it, you took it. He wanted April.

With the windows down on the truck, he enjoyed the wind on his face as he high-tailed it down the highway to Jackfish. A bottle of Wiser's Deluxe sat between his legs, the lid flung on the floor on the passenger side. He wasn't saving any for later.

Every once in a while he reached out and touched the knife on his hip and his rifle on the seat. If there was someone at Jackfish they were in for a heap of trouble. A smile played across his face. He was looking forward to hitting something. Someone. He hadn't liked her being single and had tried waiting her out. Tonight the waiting was over. If that bitch was seeing someone then there was going to be a price to pay.

He knew she was just playing hard to get again, just like back when they got married. Was that what this was about? She was trying to make him jealous? Women. He never had time for their games. He liked them in bed and in the kitchen. He should have put more time into training her. He took another long pull on the bottle.

As he made the turn onto the gravel road he felt the adrenaline mixing with the anger and the booze. She shouldn't be here now, it was way past her shift, he knew her schedule to the minute. He stopped at the top of the road and decided to turn off the engine and coast down the hill to the clearing. With the headlights off he rumbled down the road, steering back and forth between the ditches.

At the clearing he pulled off to the side and climbed out of the vehicle. He couldn't see much, but gathered his rifle and locked up the truck. Now, where were they? The old town was unliveable. Even the old stationmaster's place was a wreck. Everybody who went to high school around here had checked the place out at one time or another.

He took another shot from the bottle. Realizing it was almost empty, he tipped it up and finished it. He looked at the empty bottle for a second and then carefully set it down beside a bush.

He needed a vantage point. Then he might see some lights to guide him in. There were two hills along the train track. The first one next to the siding was the tallest. Looking up in the dark he placed the rifle over his shoulder for the steep climb.

He was moving along the hillside looking for a starting point when he noticed something in the dark. He got a little closer and his heart jumped.

Holy shit.

The vehicle was in bad shape. As Brad approached he knew it was April's cruiser. There was enough moonlight to see inside the burned-out cab. He could identify a melted radio and cop-issue laptop. What had happened here? Was she all right? He turned to the hill with renewed urgency.

Brad thought about walking around the hill to find an easy climbing spot, but figured that would be hard locate in the dark. He was a straight-on kind of guy, so he headed for the nearest part of the hill and started to go straight up. He knew he could climb.

Did this woman not see how much he wanted her? He thought back to the first time he had hit her. She had stood up to him. He still couldn't believe it. He'd come home feeling good from a night out with the boys and wanted a piece of ass. She had refused, said he was drunk. What did that have to do with anything? *Christ. Women.*

She wasn't supposed to decide when and where she would be available. Shit, she was married. She was his. Well, he put a stop to that nonsense and gave her a good hard backhand. When she began to scream at him, he slapped her again with the same hand on the way back.

Then he'd taken what he wanted and the sex had been great. She'd been a handful that night. He smiled. After that he thought things had been sorted out and she knew her place, but it had gone downhill from there.

Brad knew it was up to him to take back what was his. He reached up and pulled himself over a rock ledge. He slid down the other side only to face another rock wall, this one twice as high as the last. Brad grimaced with anger, he didn't care how high the damned rocks were. He just kept focusing on the damage he was going to do to the bastard who was messing around with his wife.

When he reached the top he became aware that there wasn't a lot of darkness left. Daybreak was close. He kept working towards the plateau where the trees were less dense. On top he liked the feel of the solid rock under his feet and brought the rifle around off his shoulder. He noticed the shelter through the trees and stopped dead. Moving his head side to side he tried to take in as much as he could, making sure there was only one.

It looked like the fencing was solid and he would make noise going over it or through it. There had to be a way in somewhere. Brad wanted to charge right in, but knew he should wait. He hoped she was okay. Was she a hostage? He could rescue her.

In fact, setting up to take her captor out when he exited the building was the smartest thing to do. Brad started circling the enclosure to find a shooting lane. The slight rise of rock behind the shelter was what he wanted. He found a bush to settle behind. The Wiser's was kicking in, but he was a better shot half-cut than most so-called experts were when they were sober.

A half hour later he heard something. Then he heard it again. He turned the rifle towards the sound and tried to make sense of it. It was coming from the tree line, not the shelter. His finger was ready, as he watched the outline of the trees in the shifting of darkness to light. Then he saw the figure.

*****

Phil was walking the trail between the two hills. He had been up all night and welcomed the first signs of daylight. The worst should be over. With the cover of darkness gone he thought the chances of an ambush were going down.

He had told April to get some rest before they went out again and she had fallen asleep. He let her nap while he went outside to keep a watch on things. That had been a hectic day for her and she'd probably never seen that kind of action before. The adrenaline crash would be enough to knock her out for a few hours. She'd be there if he needed her, and she might as well sleep while nothing was happening.

He'd checked the traps and found the guy crushed by the tree. That guy should have stayed wherever he'd come from. Phil continued to do recon in the woods for a few hours until he knew it was morning. Headed back to the shelter, he was tired and making the odd noise. He didn't think the gangsters from the camper could have got past him, so he wasn't that worried.

As he stepped into the clearing he could just make out the shelter. There was going to be a heavy fog along the shore today, already there were swirls of it hanging in the trees. Suddenly the hair on the back of his neck stood up and Phil froze.

Something was moving fast. Looking to the side he saw a blur. He only had a second to recognise the cougar as it came racing through the brush in the early light.

"Shit!"

He didn't waste time thinking, jumping backwards out of the way. He heard the gunshot while he was in the air. *What the hell?*

He landed with a thud against a tree and turned to watch the cougar streak past. It was gone in seconds. Was that a warning from the cougar, and who was shooting? Either way, it was close, he should be dead.

Phil let it go and focused on the gunshot. Then he thought of April. He couldn't sit around. He had to get her out of there. Without enough light to see clearly and he couldn't just step out into the open with a shooter around. So he crawled instead.

*****

Gunshots woke her. April scrambled off the floor while her brain reassembled the events of the night before and realized where she was. Where was Phil? Who was shooting? She grabbed her shotgun and went to the door. She wasn't sure what to do.

"Phil where are you?" She yelled.

"April, get out of there. Same place as last night. Hurry."

She didn't waste time. She didn't want to be alone inside the dome anyways. Bent over, running, she headed out the gate. She could see directly in front of her, but not much further. It wouldn't be long and it would be light out. The distance to the cliff wasn't far, but across a battlefield it seemed like a mile.

As she got to the cliff and settled behind the same rock as last night, she had no idea that she'd been seen. She gripped her shotgun tighter and wondered where Phil was. Then she heard her name.

"April, are you all right?"

Her brain hit a wall. Was that Brad?

*****

Everything was happening too fast for Brad to figure out what was going on. He was sure he'd seen a person, but then he was also sure he saw a cougar moving in the trees. His shot might have hit something, but Jesus, a cougar. He was amped up, his eyes flicking from side to side. He hadn't expected to have to watch for that.

When he saw more movement, this time by the front of the shelter, he almost took another shot. Then he thought he caught a glimpse of blond hair and reflective stripping. April. He forgot about the cougar and focused on her. She was moving into the fog out of view, away from him.

He needed to do something and yelled out, "April, are you all right?"

He waited and didn't get a response. "I know you're up here. Are you okay?"

"What are you doing here Brad?"

"I saw the burned-out truck and was worried."

"You need to get out of here Brad. Right now."

He had hoped she was in trouble and he could bail her out. Then she would respect him and do what he wanted. It didn't sound that way though. She didn't seem to want his help. "You're up here with some guy aren't you?"

She didn't respond and this time he yelled harder, "You bitch. I come up here to help you and you're with some guy. You're both dead. You hear that April?"

"Brad this is a police situation up here. Get off this damned hill and get the hell back to town."

He didn't believe a word. She was going to get it once he got his hands on her. Kill that bastard first and then have a head-to-head with her. She could scream all she wanted to out here. He smiled at the possibility. *To hell with this pissing around.* Brad stood up and started to stalk towards the shelter.

The fog was moving in and out and he'd momentarily get a good view, then everything would close up again and he'd be in the soup. He moved under the cover of fog to keep from being seen and stopped when it was clear so he could watch for anything moving.

He was standing still, waiting, about to step into the next patch of drifting fog when the granite exploded beside him and he heard the rifle shot. Brad dropped like a rock, flattening himself out on the ground.

Shit. That was a high-powered rifle, but where was it? Not nearby from the sound of it.

CHAPTER 24

Dragon waited for the fog to lift. He had moved up on to the top of the second hill while it was still dark. Fumbling around in the morning shadows he tried to find a vantage point. Then he waited.

He knew the soldier he sent up the trail would wait for light before stepping into the opening. The soldier didn't understand he was bait, meant to draw out the shooters. Dragon would sit back and take out anything that moved.

He fiddled with the scope and figured his distances. He kept getting glimpses of the other hill as the fog drifted in and out. He leaned in and married his face to the rubber ring of the scope. Something moved.

He couldn't make out who it was, but it didn't really matter. All the targets had to go down. The fog kept shifting while he tried to get the moving figure lined up. He pulled the trigger and felt the kickback. He loved that feeling, the power of the rifle.

Dragon scanned the hilltop and lost everything to another moving fog bank. They would know he was around, but he was sure no one would know where. They wouldn't be expecting a sniper. He could sit back here as the sun came up and pick them off from a distance.

The rock outcropping and the valley between the hills brought Dragon home. He felt comfortable. He was in the fight now. He had something to protect and he was going to see Tiger's mission through to the end, no matter what stood in the way.

The fog moved in his favor again and he caught sight of his soldier waiting by the trail's end. He scanned the area in front of his man and didn't see anything. He kept the scope on his man as he started to move forward into the opening crouched down, trying to stay low.

His soldier stopped and raised his gun. Dragon scanned in front of him and caught movement in the brush. He didn't have a target but he pulled the trigger anyways. The bush was good enough.

A piercing pain ripped through his calf as the rock exploded beside him and Dragon bailed, rolling off the top of the pile of boulders. He heard the return rifle shot and realized he'd been lucky. Someone did know where he was.

*****

Phil pulled the trigger. He could just barely make out the figure perched three hundred yards away on the second hill.

The first shot had come from the other side of the shelter. He was crawling towards April when he heard the second round, which had to have come from a high-powered rifle some distance away. The other hill was the only place that had the height to see the top of this hill.

He found himself a high point, a pile of boulders, and waited. He was sure he could see something there and kept his eye on the scope. He saw the flash as the sniper's second shot fired. Phil didn't hesitate and pulled the trigger. Watching the figure roll away he assumed he probably missed the guy.

Then another gunshot near the shelter caught his attention. He had to decide where to be. April's presence on top of the hill was drawing him back, but he knew the real danger was the sniper. Phil started to move towards the other hill. He needed to surprise the shooter, and began running down the trail connecting the two hills.

He didn't see the trees lining the path as he ran. Instead he saw concrete block and the brick of city alley-ways.

He banged his shoulder hard against one of the corners. The two women had worked under cover for him for the past year and now their cover was blown. He ran so hard his legs hurt. Finally he smashed through the door at the end of a skinny archway hiding the triad's safe house.

Phil knew he was losing his focus as he ran towards the second hill, but he couldn't stop the images invading his brain.

He saw the surprised look on the faces of the triad soldiers stationed inside the door as he started shooting. The man's face exploded from the close range bullet. Phil's elbow connected hard with the head of a gangster as he ran past. Someone stepped out from a room and he shot him without waiting to see if he was innocent or not. He was well past that.

*****

Brad was trying to clear his head from the booze, the confusion, and the sudden fear. There seemed to be a lot more people up here than he expected. He knew he had shot at a guy across the clearing but he was sure the bullet which almost got him had come from off to his right somewhere.

April was somewhere in front of him, maybe to the left a bit. That meant at least three of them. It was light enough now that he had a better view. He kept looking at the three places he thought had people, in front to the left, in front and somewhere far off to the right.

He caught sight of April as she adjusted her position, slipping out from behind the rock. She was hidden again, but now he knew where. When he heard something moving behind him in the tree line he started to panic. That meant four. He was getting to his knees to turn and look at the new noise when a rifle barked again.

The bullet flew through the bushes, exploding off the rock in front of him. He knew that was the long shooter. The sound of a second gunshot was closer, but no bullets came his way. What the hell was happening here? It was like he stepped into a war zone. Well, he had to keep moving in that case.

To his amazement he saw a Chinese guy crouched low coming his way. Brad couldn't understand. Was this the guy April was with? The guy looked like a criminal. *Well fuck him.* Brad stood up and they both started firing. He didn't get off the first shot, but he aimed better.

The Chinese soldier was punched backwards as the round hit him in the gut, lifting him off his feet. He landed on his ass and then his back slammed against the ground. Brad kept moving until he was standing over the guy, staring down at him. "Who the fuck are you?"

The guy's mouth was moving but he wasn't saying anything. Brad didn't care. He brought the rifle up and aimed at the man's head, then he thought better of it. "Die slowly asshole."

His heart was racing, he was pumped now. *Who was next?*

The words rang out loud and clear. "Freeze Brad, Police. Drop the gun."

*****

April quickly moved another ten feet closer. She knew the closer she got the more devastating her shotgun was. "I'm not fucking around Brad. My gun's on you now. Drop it."

"This your new man? Christ, he's a loser."

"That's just some innocent Chinese who's camping here. You just shot an innocent man Brad. You're screwed."

She watched him stand up straight. She didn't need an excuse, she had many. He had better not turn around because she wouldn't skip a beat.

"I thought you were in trouble."

"And I told you to leave. Jail time Brad, there's lots of it coming your way."

She was egging him on. He had been a problem that she didn't know how to fix, but to her amazement it looked like it was going to sort itself out. He was either going to jail or to hell, it was his choice. "Last chance Brad."

All the things he'd done to her and she'd put up with. Christ, she was getting angry all over again just thinking about it. It really was a blessing, but she was too caught up in the memories to enjoy it. She took another step forward and pumped the shotgun.

*****

Brad was scared and pissed at the same time. Fuck, he was in trouble if this guy really was just some camper. She was going to take him in. He had gotten away with a lot in the past, but she was going to take him down for this. The bitch was killing him. Didn't she realize it?

He knew there were still two more shooters out there somewhere. Were they watching? He wasn't going quietly. *Shit, he wasn't going at all.* When he heard her pump the shotgun he really didn't have any choice, she was going to have to pay.

Brad took a breath and started to dive and twist to the right.

*****

April flexed her knees, leaned into the gun and pulled the trigger. The blast left a cloud of smoke. She let it drift away and stayed still. She could hear his moaning and knew she'd got him. She felt herself start to shake. The energy seemed to seep out of her. *Was this relief?*

She wasn't sure if he still had his weapon and pumped her gun, loading another shell before she advanced slowly. She found him laid out against a rock. Her shot had been deadly from close range as she had tracked him while he dove. The left side of him was ripped apart. His arm and leg were plastered with buckshot and half of his gut was blown away.

April stopped in front of him and he stared up blankly at her.

"April."

She wasn't sure if she should shoot him again or let him die on his own. She sure as hell wasn't helping him. It went against every moral fibre in her body, but sometimes in hell you do what you have to. And he had sure made it hell.

She didn't feel anything as she stared at him. He seemed to be trying to speak. April waited him out, it seemed he was losing steam. His eyes opened wide. "I loved you April,"

"Yeah, well I hate you." She turned and walked away.

Phil was still out there fighting someone, probably the lead gangster, but she went over and sat down by the cliff. She stared out over the water, seeing her freedom for the first time.

CHAPTER 25

Dragon lost his advantage. He'd been seen. Rolling up against the edge of a sharp rock he cut his arm open. Scrambling away from the rock pile he'd been on, he looked for another high spot. He wanted to keep distance between him and the shooter he knew had to be the wild man.

Finding another elevated spot, he crawled up and peeked over the edge. He could see parts of the trail but other sections were blocked by trees and rock walls. Something was moving fast in his direction. He tried to watch through the scope and caught enough of the running figure to know he'd been right.

The guy was running, open for mere seconds at a time. Dragon needed to slow him down even if he missed. He sighted on the next opening and put slight pressure on the trigger. The first hint of the runner and he finished the squeeze. One shot, a quick pull later and a second bullet was on its way.

He saw the tree explode and his target jump off the trail into the woods. At least he knew which side of the trail he was on. The guy wouldn't be running anymore. Now the question was should he stay put, or move to intercept? He closed his eyes and let his instincts take over.

This was a killing time.

He could still see his first victim. His father had caught a smuggler who was stealing some of their product and selling it on the side. After beating the man nearly to death he'd called Dragon over. He could still see the questioning look on his father's face. "This man tries to steal the food from our table. He wants us to suffer. What should we do with him?"

He'd been unsure what to say until his father handed him the machete. He'd swung them before at trees and vines, but now he held it with both hands and felt its power. He realized what his father wanted and knew he understood the message. "No one takes what belongs to the family. Not without sacrifice."

Dragon stepped forward and started to swing the machete. Most of his father's men turned their backs and walked away because of the mess he was making, but his father stayed at his side until he finally connected with a fatal blow. Killing had come easy the first time, and he had done better with the machete as he gained more practice.

He opened his eyes and scanned the forest through the scope. He didn't think the wild man would have had time to see where he was and this was a good place to settle and wait.

*****

Phil's instinct drove him off the trail and back to the present. He landed rolling and slammed up against a tree.

Shit that hurt.

He collected himself and stopped to think. He'd seen the flash out of the corner of his eye as he left the trail. The shot had come from over by the cliffs on the other hill. The guy had a good shooting lane.

"Waiting, huh?"

Phil eased himself backwards into the woods, he wasn't going forward along this line. He went back ten yards and eased up to the trail again. He was taking a chance, but thought it was worth it. He crawled across the trail and into the woods on the other side.

Now he could work his way through the slight valley between hills and hope the shooter thought he was somewhere on the other side. Phil stayed in the thickest underbrush and pushed himself along as quietly as he could.

He was working his way up the second hill knowing he had to be getting closer because of the steep upwards slope. When he came to an opening he crawled to the edge and pointed his rifle out in front. Slowly he moved the scope back and forth combing the hill inch by inch looking for anything.

He was pretty sure that from this angle he wasn't going to find much, but then he caught sight of a patch of color against the grey rock and focused in.

"There you are."

He could make out a boot and was sure the guy was lying down on the flattened top of a boulder pointing towards the trail. It wasn't a long shot, but there was very little target available. He took his time with this one, he wanted it to count. He let out a slow breath and squeezed the trigger. The gun jumped, but he kept his eye to the scope and watched for damage.

He saw a leg jerk and thought he'd scored a hit. He was ready for the guy to sit up and expose himself further. That was the usual response. Once they were hit they forgot about the danger and worried about their lives. When they exposed themselves they ensured the wound was converted into a kill.

Phil wasn't that lucky, or the guy was skilled and knew better. Either way the shooter went forward off the rock and all Phil saw was a boot sliding out of sight.

"Gotcha."

Phil didn't waste a second. He was up and running towards the top. He had to capitalize on his prey's wound and get the guy before he went to ground.

His brain was flashing pictures again.

He could see the hallway with door after door to choose from. He didn't know which one to pick, but every second was critical. What was the room number? He couldn't remember. He reloaded his pistols as he ran.

The door at the end of the hallway had no number. What? Putting his shoulder out he charged. He heard people running behind him as he crashed into the room, falling, his momentum rolling him across the floor. He came up shooting and at least two of them went down.

Phil stopped. He realized he was standing on the top of a hill in the middle of nowhere firing his rifle blindly. He didn't even have a target. He was losing it at the worst possible time. He had to stay in the present. Focus on the now. He'd just lost any advantage he had by announcing himself.

"Wake the fuck up Phil. Jesus."

Since he'd run right past the shooter's hiding spot he turned around and returned to look for a blood trail.

"Bingo."

There was a spatter of rusty red on the back of the boulder where he had seen the foot. Well, it should be easier now, but then there was nothing worse than an injured animal. So he wouldn't rush into anything.

Scanning the ground quickly he found the first blood spot and then a second. The line went right into the woods. Tracking a wounded animal was just a matter of making sure you didn't get close enough for it to strike back. Tracking a wounded gangster who had a weapon was suicidal, especially in the thick trees.

"What now?"

There was no waiting, he felt the impulse to run again, his head swirling. He stepped into the woods and began to stalk the shooter.

Then he was looking at the two men he'd shot lying on the floor. He bolted through the entrance to the living room and stopped in horror.

The laughter made him turn his head. The Triad leader sat on a couch with a pair of women kneeling at his feet. He wore nothing but a towel wrapped around his waist. Phil couldn't keep his eyes away from the corner of the room. He felt his world crumbling as he shook with disgust.

The laughter made him look sideways again. The gangster was openly mocking him, rubbing his face in what had happened here. Phil stepped towards the corner, he couldn't register the sight, but the voices in his brain knew this was bad. He felt his head get light and he thought he was going to pass out. Then he heard the words.

"Too late detective. You caused this."

*****

He had never been hurt before, not seriously. The pain was excruciating. Knowing the shot came from below he'd pulled himself forward off the front of the rock. Needing some space, he went right into the woods. Dragon crashed through forest until he found a small protected notch in a fractured rock face and finally came to a stop. He had to wrap his leg and stop the bleeding.

He also had to make a decision. There were only a few rounds left for the rifle. He knew it would run out if it came to a battle. He decided to hide it under some brush and pulled his knife out. For the first time he had fears about getting to his wealth.

He was thinking of Tiger and wondering what happened to him. Did he die fighting for the secret? Did he realize it was slipping away? Dragon was shaking he was so angry. This wild man had to die. It was his destiny to find the wealth and he was going to succeed, or die trying.

He started to look for something on the forest floor. When he found it he started looking for a place to set his trap. He undid the cloth around his leg and used some of his own blood to set things up. The waiting would be the hard part. Dragon sat hidden in the underbrush, centering himself, drifting back to the Chinese mountains.

He hoped the wild man found him sooner than later. He flexed his fingers and squeezed his hand around the handle of the knife.

*****

Phil was following the signs, broken branches and flattened brush on autopilot, as though he was somewhere else.

He heard the words of the Triad leader as the images in the corner formed into real beings in his head. Body parts were piled on a large piece of plastic, blood pooling on the sheet. There were too many legs and arms for one person, and his gut said it was the two women who worked for him.

The weight of guilt was too much to hold and he slammed his brain shut on the picture of the women. He was close to screaming, the fury mounting like acid in his throat. He looked at his shaking hands clenched around the guns.

The ground shifted around Phil and he refocused on the woods. The leaves exploded beside him and he swung his rifle defensively. He caught a glint of light as the knife came up from the ground and the butt of his rifle connected just in time to deflect the blow.

Phil jumped back trying to organize his vision. The blood track had been laid out right past the spot where the gangster was hiding. He'd walked right into the trap.

Shithead.

The Chinese gangster rolled forwards even as Phil backed away. Then he was up and lunging. Phil pulled the trigger with one hand on the rifle as he reached for the machete on his waist with the other. He felt the weight of the man slamming into him as he was knocked backwards.

The gun bounced free and fell to the side. He didn't mind, he was focused on the handle of the machete, squeezing his fingers around it as he stepped sideways to avoid the next attack.

He felt his senses shut down as he turned and opened up with the two guns. The Triad boss stopped laughing, but it was too late. One of his lieutenants jumped in front of him, but went down fast with a pair of bullets in his chest.

Phil pumped three into the leader and two more into another lieutenant. He could see the shock in the leader's face. He never expected a cop to start shooting unarmed people. That was against the law.

Phil didn't give a shit anymore. He pulled the triggers until there were no more bullets and then he stuffed in two new magazines. He held off anyone who came near the room until he eventually heard the sirens in the distance.

A sharp pain in his leg broke his trance and he looked down.

"You bastard."

Phil's reaction was to raise the machete and drive it down on the hand still holding the knife. He watched the hand recoil before he connected and the machete struck the ground.

Stepping back he reached down to pull the knife out of his thigh. He should leave it in, but if he did the gangster might grab it again so he threw it over his shoulder into the bush. The Chinese was already up and running at him.

Phil knew he was going to get hit again and couldn't move his feet. He did lift his arms and thrust forward as the gangster hit, feeling the machete blade sink in as they went over backwards. Phil shifted in the air, trying not to land on the bottom, and they hit the ground side by side.

He looked into the gangster's eyes as they lay there two feet apart, locked together by the machete. His opponent tried to change positions and Phil rammed the blade in further. The guy jerked in pain and stopped trying to move. Phil could see desperation in the man's eyes. He started to yell and scream at Phil in Chinese, but the words meant nothing.

For some reason Phil yelled back,

"Fuck you asshole. Fuck you."

He didn't have the energy to move and he didn't want to loosen his grip on the machete handle. He knew the man was dying and would just wait him out.

As he studied the man's tormented face he sensed there was a lot more going on with this Chinese than it appeared. The guy looked heartbroken, it didn't seem to be because he was about to die. He kept looking off into the forest and waving his hand to the west as if he wanted to go in that direction, which made no sense to Phil. There was nothing that way but the railroad track, another hill, and endless miles of wilderness.

CHAPTER 26

April got down behind the rocks at the edge of the cliff when she heard the rifle shots. She'd been worried for the last hour. She wanted to get up and move, but had to admit she was scared and would wait a bit longer. Instead she occupied her time making lists of what she had to do. Collect bodies and get word into town were at the top.

"April."

She recognised Phil's voice. "Here."

"Everything okay?"

"Well everything's dead here if that's what you mean."

"Same thing."

She noticed the limp and could see where he had wrapped his leg. He was covered in scratches that she assumed were from the forest, otherwise he seemed okay. "Anyone left over there?"

"No, just a few by the camper, but they aren't fighters."

"Okay, we need to collect those men and get out of here. I'll have to take you in."

"I know." He sat on the ground. It was going to be a long day.

*****

The train's engineer sat up in his seat. What was that? Something on the track. He was used to animals, but this seemed strange. As he got closer he became sure it was a person, he leaned on the train's air horns.

The person kept waving their arms for him to stop. These people didn't seem to know that these trains were run remotely by computers. In reality he was just a passenger who wasn't supposed to touch the controls unless told to. The closer he got the more adamant the arm waver seemed to become.

He had no choice but to slow the train down, and he had to start quickly because this thing took a long time to stop. As the slowing train got closer he got a better look at the waving female and then noticed the others off to the side. Shit, he thought to himself, that looks like a cop. The locomotive didn't quite stop in time, rolling twenty feet past her. He waited for her to come up beside his engine, looking down at her from the open doorway.

"We need a ride into Schreiber. "

He'd seen a lot, but this was a first. Who was he to say no? It was against regulations, but shit, she had a shotgun in her hands. "Sure thing, climb up."

*****

The Chinese worker couldn't believe he was really going to make it home to his family in Vancouver. He knew he shouldn't have taken the envelope in his hand, he stared down at it wondering about the address. The Chang family, China. When the cop said the trailer was being left behind he had taken a quick look. Now he hoped that getting it to the family could be advantageous to him. Quickly he stuffed the envelope inside his jacket and reached up for the train conductor's hand.

*****

Two months later everything was quiet in the old ghost town of Jackfish. Phil spent some time in jail until things were sorted out. Eventually he had been released and recognised for helping April in the situation.

He returned to his daily routine and started to pile wood for the winter. Two things had changed though. First, he didn't seem to be flashing back to the past as often as he used to. He knew visions of Chinese gangsters and triad tattoos were going to be with him forever, but he was living better now and he was looking forward, not inward.

He'd finally accepted what he'd done and decided he could find a way to live with it. It was the past now and would stay there. If anything, this whole situation solidified his views on his old job and his life in the city.

He was home now and would make a go of it here.

The second thing had been the discovery. He'd taken the time to work through it all again and replayed the whole set of events in his head. Something hadn't made sense. Where had the other gangster disappeared to?

Phil saw him head into the woods with his boss that day. When the leader came back he'd been alone.

The curiosity built until he couldn't ignore it any more. Phil ventured down the rail line, past the first two hills, to the spot he thought they had disappeared and started to look around. It didn't take long to find the broken twigs along the track they had made. Their trail went in behind the third hill where he got slowed up by the thick trees. It was easier to follow with all the broken branches now and he could see their path clearly.

When he came to the rock wall at the back of the hill he stopped and looked around. He realized that the pile of loose wood on the ground had been moved recently and reached down to lift some branches off the stack. Strange, but it looked like the pile was hiding fresh dirt.

He decided to examine the other pile of wood leaning up against the rock face. Grabbing it with both arms, he moved the pile to the side, leaving it standing up. The view knocked him right on his ass and he sat there for an hour staring at it.

Was the gangster here for this? How the hell would he know it was here? Phil looked back at the fresh dirt on the ground behind him.

Maybe that would provide an answer.

*****

April knew she was taking a gamble but thought it was worth it. She walked up the trail to the top of the first hill. She'd been up to visit him a number of times since the incident. She liked his company and he didn't tell her to get lost, at least not yet.

He had cleaned up pretty well, the haircut and shave had done wonders. Even with nothing to take your focus away you ended up getting sucked into those eyes. She really liked those eyes — well — the rest was pretty good too.

Winter was close. The smoke coming out the top of the shelter and the woodpile confirmed it. She wanted to force the situation. "Hey there, anyone home?" She stood outside the gate.

He came to the large window opening at the front of the shelter and waved her in. Inside they settled on the small chairs he'd built.

"Thought I'd come visit for the weekend if you didn't mind?" All the other visits had ended when she had returned to town at the end of the day. This time she planned to spend the night.

His eyebrows rose, then he smiled and pointed to the bags on the floor. "All right then, you can help me figure out what that's worth."

She reached forward, curious. Her hand came back out of the bag with a pile of worn and dirty bills. She was confused. Turning them over in her hands, it was pretty obvious they were old. She'd never seen them before, but the dates on the bills sure stood out. "What's this?"

"It's a story that's bigger than us." He stopped for a moment. "I think someone hid these bills here a long time ago. I'm willing to bet our Chinese friend was here to get them. Don't ask me how he knew, but I think he did."

"How much is this stuff worth today?"

"There's five thousand dollars in one and two dollar bills. They're all eighteen-eighty Dominion dollars. My guess is probably two or three hundred for each bill."

"Shit Phil, that's one and a half million."

"Yup, I figure it's ours."

She hadn't come for money. She was looking for something else and stood up, reaching her hand out. He grabbed it and she pulled him up. She was being aggressive here and moved in close to look up into his eyes. When he reached down, picked her up and turned for the bed she agreed. He should be the aggressor.

EPILOGUE

Phil stumbled from the bed and pulled on some trousers, hunting along the floor for socks. He looked beside the stove for a stick of wood but there wasn't any. Throwing on a coat, he glanced at the bed. He knew what they meant by the song, "I feel gooood…"

She was right out, blanket pulled up to her chin, hair falling across her face, he liked the look. He decided that more than anything he wanted back in there with her and hurried to the door. He thought of the money briefly as he walked past the bag full of bills sitting on the floor. He thought about the gold as he walked across the yard. She didn't need to know about it. Nobody did.

The lightning bolt of white quartz in the granite wall had a solid line of gold running through the middle. He wondered if the inch-thick vein was wider inside the rock. Either way, he didn't want any mining happening here. He wanted it just the way it was. The gold was there if he ever needed it and he was pretty sure no one else knew about it.

Smiling, Phil threw open the gate and headed to the woodpile.

Everything happened at once. A blur of black moved from his right and he glanced that way just in time to see the bear racing across the clearing. He didn't have his gun.

"Oh shit."

He sensed motion from his left. Phil felt more than saw the cougar fly by his head. He thought he smelled it, he was sure he heard it. The cougar growled as he rushed in to attack the bear, they rolled once and stood up on their hind legs trading shots. The bear wasn't serious enough to want to fight the cat and backed off.

Phil stood, frozen to the ground, mesmerized. The cougar stood there panting while Phil shook. It looked at him and let out a small grunting sound. The two of them stood there for a second longer, although it seemed an hour. Finally he figured it out.

"Okay, big fella, we're even."

He felt comfortable to turn his back on the cougar and head back to his shelter. The small dome seemed a lot more inviting than usual. The place seemed to be coming alive. *Hell, if April moved in this place won't be a ghost town any more. It'll be like Jackfish reborn.*

The End.

Book reviews help readers decide if a particular book is right for them. They also help writers by providing practical feedback on what you liked about the book. If you enjoyed this book, please take a moment to write down a few words describing what you liked about Jackfish Reborn at your favourite book retailer or at Goodreads, and help spread the word.

JACKFISH NOW

The ghost town of Jackfish May/2013
Photo — Peggy Ireland

All that's left after the fire at the old hotel is the granite stone foundation.
May/2013   *Photo — Peggy Ireland*

CP Rail line through the rock cut at the east end of Jackfish siding, May/2013   *Photo – Peggy Ireland*

About the Author

Rejean Giguere is an avid outdoorsman, adventurer, photographer and artist. He enjoys fishing, hockey, golf, tennis, skiing and snowmobiling, his V-Max motorcycle and vintage Corvette.

He grew up in Canada and Europe, and enjoyed a business career in Toronto and Ottawa.

Visit his website at www.rejeangiguere.com

Enjoy this sample of my novel Endpoint.

ENDPOINT

an endpoint is the entry point to a service, a process, or a queue or topic destination

PROLOGUE

Chantal stood at the door, one hand on her hip, the other hand holding up a cigarette, a small trail of smoke rising upwards. No smoking bylaws for her. Now there was another look he'd seen before. The head cocked slightly to the side, the raised eyebrow saying it all. *Are we done yet?*

Gary hid a grin and headed towards her. She was sexy when she was mad but she didn't need to know that. Besides, it was an extra bonus whenever he got her going. She'd agreed to come all the way down from Manhattan to Brooklyn for the meeting so he figured he ought to get her back now that it was over. "Come on sweetie, it wasn't that bad was it?"

She didn't even answer; she took a drag on the stick, turned on her heel and stalked out the door with a little extra emphasis on the strut. She didn't know it, but it was this type of stuff that made her so damned sexy when she was mad.

Gary followed her out the door grinning from ear to ear.

CHAPTER 1

Chantal pushed open the door at the bottom of the stairs. Turning left, she headed along 50th Street's mix of shops and homes. There was everything from delivery trucks to motorbikes parked along the curb. Patches of light and shadow broke up the sidewalk under the trees. Gary was a few feet behind her, lengthening his steps to catch up, when all hell broke loose.

As Chantal's heels clicked against the concrete a shadow stepped out from behind a tree and fell in behind her. The guy was between them now. As Gary started to speed up, trying to get to her, the guy lunged forward and grabbed her around the neck. At the same instant he saw another attacker coming off the street from where he had been crouched between a pair of cars.

Changing course, Gary headed for this new attacker. In the back of his head he knew Chantal could defend herself, at least until he got there. Time slowed, his mental training took over, he kept walking forward, knowing it would take about four more steps to intercept. He glanced over to see Chantal as she dropped down, pulling on the attacker who had his hands around her neck. Using her assailant's own momentum, while twisting, she sent the guy over her head towards the pavement.

Gary focused on the second attacker who had changed direction and was now coming directly at him.

The guy looked big and carried himself confidently. Wading in he threw a left jab. Gary didn't hesitate or step back. Instead he stepped forward, inside the punch, simultaneously grabbing the guy's arm by the wrist, gripping a handful of jacket and pivoting his hip into the guy's stomach.

Gary already had the guy off balance and just like Chantal, he dropped down and using the man's momentum, propelled him right over top. Unlike Chantal, Gary wasn't kidding around. As the guy flew towards the pavement, he shifted again, getting a solid grip on the attacker's arm, lifting upwards hard as the guy fell.

The crack, pop and scream all came together as the guy's shoulder dislocated and his arm broke leaving the man groaning on the street. Then Gary took the time to look at Chantal circling with her attacker. The man looked a little more cautious now. *Good girl, you're buying some time.* A commotion behind them caught Gary's attention and he swivelled to see what was happening.

The tough looking black dude from the meeting they had just left was fighting someone else about twenty yards behind them. What the hell was going on? Gary started processing information as he headed towards Chantal. This was a crew, these guys looked big and strong. Organized.

Who was the black guy from the meeting? And what side was he on? Gary had noticed him sitting off to the side at the migraine support group.

It seemed like they were after Chantal. No matter, it was stopping here. Chantal's opponent had her down and was wrestling with her from above. Gary never broke stride, coming in with a hard driving knee into the guy's ribs.

The force lifted the man in black right off Chantal and sent him tumbling. Gary was right there, following. As the attacker stopped rolling he came up holding a gun. Gary froze as his brain tried to catch up. Guns? If they had guns why wait until now? Why not pull them at the beginning? Something was off here, but there was no time to work on it. He needed to disarm this asshole.

Just then, a black van squealed to a stop. Men jumped out as the driver started yelling at the gunman who was staring Gary down. He recognized the language. Russian. *What the hell?*

Gary saw the attacker turn his eyes towards the van's driver and took two quick steps forward, inside the gunman's arm. One hand grabbed the wrist with the gun, while his other elbow swung hard, hitting the guy solidly on the jaw, leaving him completely dazed. Before the guy fell backwards Gary grabbed his wrist with both hands.

As the attacker fell his wrist snapped backwards, broken. Squealing, he dropped the weapon to the concrete. Gary kicked the gun down the sidewalk and looked around. He felt his heart pounding and knew he was in full gear, everything moving in slow motion. He saw more men coming from the van in a run, the driver climbing out.

The black guy from the meeting seemed to be looking at Gary expectantly while leaning over his beaten rival. Lastly, he saw the shock on Chantal's face. It was clearly time to go.

"Run!" He pushed Chantal towards the dark space between two houses before grabbing her hand, taking the lead. He had no idea what was going on, but was sure they would lose this battle if they stayed on the street. Since he didn't know how many more attackers there were, running up the sidewalk made no sense.

*****

"What's going on?" Chantal yelled as she ran behind Gary. He wasn't answering and that wasn't a good sign. *Jesus Christ, what the hell was going on?* Suddenly they were in the alley between the two buildings. She was agile but Gary was really pulling her and she fought to stay upright.

Grass below her feet meant they were in a backyard. He didn't slow down, just kept pulling her into the darkness behind the house. When he stopped and turned, he pointed to the high fence. Grabbing her around the waist, he lifted her up, "Over the fence! Go!" She kicked into gear and found the top of the fence, pulling herself up and over.

She didn't have to wait long, Gary dropped down beside her. "These guys aren't fucking around, we give it everything. Right now."

Chantal jumped up and ran with him.

He was going to save her again, which was crazy because that was how they'd met.

A couple years before she'd made the mistake of stepping out the back door of a bar to have a smoke instead of going out the front. Some real assholes were hanging out there and next thing you knew things were getting out of hand. One of them grabbed her ass and she'd pulled away. Then another had said, "Come on baby, we'll be easy on you. You don't want to get hurt do you?"

She'd started running towards the street, but one guy was on her pretty quick, yelling, "Hey guys, give me a hand here, we can't let her go yet." He caught her, laughing as he wrapped her up in his arms and picked her off the ground. Chantal bit his hand and made sure she landed on his feet when he dropped her. By then the others caught up and they'd swarmed her. That was when a guy walking by the alley heard her scream. He'd been just walking by, but his timing had been perfect.

Chantal saw him stop and turn. He'd taken half a second to realize a woman was in some sort of trouble. He didn't hesitate, running down the alley. The other guys took one look at him, tall and slender, and thought he was going to provide a little bonus entertainment. One of them held Chantal while the other two moved towards the intruder.

She watched him take on the two assholes and hurt them both. One was left nursing a couple broken bones, while the other was out cold. When she felt the hold on her arm ease, she had chopped down on the guy still holding her and broke his hold, running towards the guy who'd saved her. The third guy wasted no time running the other way down the alley. Suddenly it was just the two of them standing there.

"Hi, my name's Gary, Gary Collins."

He'd been so calm that night, and every other night for three years now. But back then it amazed her how someone so calm could unleash such devastation; it still amazed her today.

They ran by the front of a house and straight across the road, around the back of another. Chantal knew that Gary had seen the van too, as it slid around the corner of the street and tried to cut them off before they crossed. *Not this time asshole,* she thought. Gary kept pulling her along as he swerved around things, jumping small obstacles.

In the next back yard they turned left and ran towards the neighbors on the side instead of climbing the back fence. Again, they scrambled over the top of a six foot brick wall into a garden. Before she could stop to catch her breath, Gary landed beside her, "Go!"

He motioned, and away they went again. They heard someone hit the wall they'd just cleared. Chantal was in the lead now, vaulting herself over the small wooden fence of the next yard. She didn't look back, heading for the next fence.

Gary caught up and pointed back out towards the road they had crossed. Ducking between the cars along the curb, they looked quickly both ways before running back across the street and into yet another back yard. Chantal saw the logic, double back, the van would be one street away expecting them to continue that direction. Turning back ensured the van was out of the picture momentarily at least. They could see the guy following them on foot had figured out their plan as a tall long-limbed, black-dressed, figure started across the street on the same line.

"Keep going over fences in that direction until I catch up." Gary pushed her and she didn't hesitate. The first fence was small enough to clear easily. Then she heard Gary and the attacker start fighting as she ran across the yard. The next one was a brick wall, she jumped up and caught the edge, then kept working her feet on the wall until she was able to grab more of the top. She looked back before she dropped over the wall and saw someone's dark silhouette coming across the yard after her.

Was it Gary? She was already scared. The next couple of fences were small enough that she didn't slow down. When the person chasing her was close enough to reach out and grab her, Chantal turned to defend herself, only to be tackled backwards. She was about to start kicking and punching when she heard, "Hey there sexy, don't be so feisty, we don't have time for that kind of stuff. "

"What the hell are you knocking me down for?"

"Because you were going to hit me. Am I right? Well I just did it gently. You weren't going to be so careful. Now let's sit here a second." She wanted a cigarette, could feel a migraine coming on, and what did he want to do? *He wanted to sit a minute.*

*****

Gary knew they couldn't keep running through backyards. It was time for the next course of action. They'd created separation, now they needed to lay low somewhere. Since they were near the bottom of Brooklyn and he didn't know the area, he wasn't sure where to go. They'd come down from Manhattan to South Ferry and then across the mouth of the East River. In Brooklyn they'd come down the Culver Line right into Coney Island and then walked a short way to the meeting. They were well off track now.

Gary was trying to orientate himself, figure out where he was, and where the closest transit station was. He could see Chantal was a little rattled but hanging in there. That was okay, he was too. Silently he motioned for her to follow as they headed towards the street stopping between a bush and the fence dividing the next property.

"We'll wait here for a bit, okay?" He could tell that it wasn't okay by the look on her face.

"Here? Are you for real?" she whispered.

He wasn't sure. He wanted to let time go by, hoping the attackers would have to spread out their search zone. They weren't going back towards the meeting place or the station they'd gotten off at. He wanted to head away from the meeting site, and out of the containment circle. Time was his friend. So they sat.

He was feeling guilty because the migraine meeting had been his idea. He had hoped that listening to other's symptoms and descriptions of their auras would be helpful to Chantal. He had learned a lot of new things about how migraines worked by listening to the others, like the one who said his headaches started as a slow pulse in the back of his neck, pushing up into his brain, settling a throb in his right temple. Then the throb increased until it was like an ice pick stabbing into his brain.

A long half-hour later he got what he was waiting for. A black van turned the corner of the block and came slowly down the street. Gary pulled Chantal under the bushes with him. He listened as the van rolled by and felt Chantal's fingers sinking into his arm. Okay, the attackers cleared this street and would be off to the next. He kept the two of them there another fifteen minutes.

Without a word the pair started walking south. They were fully alert as they neared the end of the block. Once across the street, still walking south, it was hard to ignore the urge to keep looking back. Reading the Russian writing on the signs above the stores Gary realized they must be getting close to Brighton

Beach, a well known Russian community. He had a number of thoughts at once. He might even have a plan.

Watching the storefronts, he searched for something, finally finding it on the next block. The sign would mean nothing to Chantal, but Gary translated the Russian, "The Old Man's Hole". A bar would do just fine.

CHAPTER 2

Chantal was totally confused when Gary stopped in front of a dingy bar and pulled open the door. What the hell was he doing now. *Christ, hasn't this been enough for one night.* She stepped into the bar and went from darkness into blackness.

This wasn't like any bar she was used to. Where were the lights and loud music? This place was all dark; tiny lamps lit small tables where men huddled in the shadows. She couldn't even see the unused tables if the lamps weren't lit. No one sat at the bar along the back. She wondered where the bartender was.

She stopped next to Gary, then jumped when something moved beside her. The man standing there in the shadows seemed to be a waiter. Chantal watched as Gary spoke to him in a foreign language. The waiter turned and led them to one of the small tables near the back and switched on a little lamp.

When Chantal sat down she couldn't see Gary's face, just his chest and neck. It reminded her of an old black and white mobster movie.

She looked at the table next to them and noticed at least two men's heads were turned her way. *Jesus, this place is supposed to be safe?*

"Gary, what in the hell are we doing in here?" she whispered, leaning forward.

"I need to think."

"In this place?" He was so goddamned calm that it irritated her, but he was deep in thought so she let him go. The waiter came and before she could open her mouth, Gary answered. All she understood was Vodka. Well, that would do and she settled back in her chair. She took a deep breath and realized she was smelling tobacco. Looking around she saw the odd glare of red tips in the dark. Thank god. Think all you want Gary. She started fishing in her purse for a pack.

"What language are you speaking?"

"Russian."

Chantal was going to have to ask more questions about this Russian connection. Back when they started dating he'd mentioned living there or something, but not much more. The waiter was obviously the bartender too, he brought some vodka in shot glasses. Chantal slapped the first one down wanting to calm her nerves. She sipped the second and had another cigarette while she watched Gary do his thinking.

She shouldn't have let him talk her into going to the damned meeting. Through the whole thing all she could think was that it was a waste of time. She couldn't wait to get out of there. But she could tell that he had been in to it, he'd even gone up to speak to the doctor after it was over. Analyzing, calculating and digesting, wasn't that what he said one time?

Now it was like he was making a decision, she could see the struggle on his face. He seemed to be wrestling with his next step. She knew he'd finally made a decision when he finished his shot, smiled at her, and waved the waiter over with a couple more.

He got out his cell phone and looked through his contacts. She saw the hesitation before Gary finally dialled.

*****

The number had been with him for ages. Even when it changed over the years he was always notified. He'd never called the number and hadn't seen it's owner in twenty years. The most recent change was to a New York exchange. He wished he didn't have to call it now, but after thinking about it, and the danger that was clearly there for Chantal, he knew what he had to do.

Someone answered the phone in Russian. "Ya, kto tam?"

"I want to speak to Ivan."

"Ivan, Ivan who? Who is this?"

Gary wasn't planning to play games, "Look, I'm only going to say this once, I need Ivan Petrovski. Now. You tell him Gary is calling."

Gary knew the Russian would be confused. His job was probably just to screen calls. He wouldn't want to compromise his boss, but would definitely not recognise this caller. The fact Gary had dropped Ivan's last name would be the clincher, this Russian might not even know it himself. The guy would become concerned about doing the wrong thing with someone that knew Ivan personally.

Finally the Russian muttered, "Wait a minute."

*****

Ivan Petrovski sat in the back of one of the many buildings his numbered company owned. The Sambo martial arts training centre fronted onto the street. In the back, through a guarded door, there was an open warehouse with a training area to one side. Work benches took up the left side. The centre was open enough for the few trucks parked there.

Ivan had become a criminal while a youngster in Russia. He'd worked his way up through the neighborhood gangs and then into the Russian mob before leaving during the breakup of the country. He eventually settled down in the Russian section of Brooklyn. Fifteen years later his fingers were into everything in this section of town, his enterprises stretching out across parts of the U.S. and back to his homeland.

Tonight he was relaxing, watching two of his men train while he played chess with another. He ought to go home to either his wife or girlfriend early tonight, but he always enjoyed the camaraderie of being with his men. He yelled at one of the men training, "No Nickolas, don't twist and try to throw. You must throw and then twist. Try again."

One of his guards let in someone carrying a phone who headed right for his table. Ivan didn't like interruptions, that's why he didn't carry the phone. He took a reading of the messengers face. The man wasn't supposed to come in unless it was important. His look was one of confusion.

"This better be important because I don't have the time." He reached forward and moved his knight.

The messenger leaned much closer than usual and whispered. "The man on the phone said your last name was Petrovski, which I cannot confirm sir. He said his name was Gary"

At the mention of his last name Ivan became concerned, with reason. It wasn't a name known in America. He had made sure it was untraceable. But the second that he heard Gary's name, he was intrigued.

Gary Collins — well — it had been a long time. He felt the adrenaline start trickling into his veins. Whenever he was around it meant things always got interesting. The two of them were like lightning rods.

Ivan waved everyone out of the room. He poured himself a shot from the open bottle of Vodka beside the chess board to help clear his thoughts before he raised the phone.

"Ivan here." He answered in Russian.

"Gary Collins. Is it a bad time?"

"For you, an old friend, there is always time." He was extremely curious. He didn't know what this was about, and any contact from the past could go either way. "Although I wish this was a call to catch up on old times, I assume you're calling for a reason?"

"I need your help. I wouldn't call unless it was urgent. I think I'm in your neighborhood and I'm being followed."

Ivan could hear the stress in his old friend's voice, but there was also the calmness and clarity he remembered. He knew Gary could handle himself and wondered why he needed help. As a second thought he wondered who was chasing him and why.

"The Gary Collins I knew wouldn't be needing much help. What's going on?"

"That's the problem. These people aren't after me. They're after my girlfriend. We were on 50th street trying to get back to the subway when a professional crew, that had a van and five or six Russian speaking guys, tried to grab her. I decided to run when they showed their guns."

Ivan wasn't expecting that. Gary was only asking help for the woman. He didn't want her hurt. Five or six guys with guns really was too much for any unarmed man. They were lucky to have gotten away.

"What do you want me to do?" He knew that if Gary was on the phone, he already knew what he needed.

"I don't know your business, but I assume that you have some muscle. Can we get an escort to the B train?"

That was probably an easy assumption. This was a simple request. It didn't sound like there was anything here, just a bit of help required. "Of course. Tell me where you are and my men will come and get you. Tell them where you want to go and they will take you. They can even drive you home if you wish."

"A ride to the train would be a big help Ivan. Thank you." Gary nodded over at Chantal. "We're at The Old Man's Hole, a small bar south of 50th. Do you know it?"

Ivan was impressed, he knew the bar. It was a smoky side street place where older men discussed business deals. It was a good place for quiet meetings and a good place to hide in the darkness. "Yes, I know where it is. I'm in the middle of some business right now," he moved a pawn, "but I do want to know more about these Russians you ran into, so please fill in my men when they get there."

"Okay, but you make sure your men announce themselves when they approach, we're not kidding around here."

Ivan heard the warning and understood the danger to his men. He knew exactly what Gary could do. "Okay, they're on their way. I hope I can help. You owe me a dinner for this you know, so I hope to see you soon."

"Thanks Ivan, I just want to get through the night. I do owe you one, take care."

Ivan closed the cell phone and stared at it for a moment. Shaking himself out of it, he jumped off his chair yelling towards the front of the building. As men came running in to the back room he started issuing orders. He gave the senior man specific instructions. Then he watched as his crew geared up, loaded a truck and left through the garage doors at the back of the building.

*****

Gary looked around the bar, they weren't getting much more attention than when they came in. He knew the men were looking at Chantal. That happened. With her long legs and long black hair she was hard to miss. They both relaxed. Chantal had another cigarette and a number of shots. He downed his own shots with the comfort that came from knowing a plan was in motion.

Now he had time to review the earlier meeting. The part that fascinated him was when people started describing auras. They seemed to settle into two types, one group had blank spots, the other had objects laid over top of their vision. He was surprised that Chantal finally spoke up at the end, describing the line she got during a migraine that ran right through the middle of her vision. It was clearly different that everybody else's.

Ten minutes later two scrawny guys came in. Gary's first thought was meth heads. Their dirty clothes looked like they hadn't been changed in weeks. He hoped that they didn't get by the waiter but watched cash change hands and the two walked in. *Local dealers with cash to burn.* He eased his chair back slightly into the darkness.

The two made their way to the bar at the back, coming within ten feet of Gary and Chantal's table. Everything seemed fine while the new arrivals had a quick beer and a shot. They were on their second beer and shot when they took notice of Chantal. It was possible they thought they were looking at an easy score, but Gary knew it was more likely Chantal that caught their attention.

One of them spoke up in heavily accented English. "Hey there sexy woman, you want to join with two real men for a drink?"

Gary barely shook his head, warning her not to react. Chantal kept her eyes on him. He knew she would follow his lead, she was experienced enough to be able to ignore a couple of mouthy drunks.

The cocky one decided to push it further, walking over to their table. Standing on the other side of Chantal he asked her again, "You want to come with real men? You could leave this piece of shit," he pointed across the little table.

Gary answered for her in Russian. "The next five minutes could be bad for you. Not a threat, just something to consider."

He watched the guy thinking about that. The dealer looked quickly around the room. He was calculating whatever danger there was, and to him the consequences didn't seem high. He finally smiled and turned to his buddy, "Hey, this shit wants some trouble, can you believe it?"

His friend pulled a knife as he came towards the table, but didn't get far.

The front doors swung open and three heavily tattooed men moved swiftly through. The first intercepted the waiter coming from his regular spot in the shadows. The waiter took one look at the intensity on the man's face and stopped dead. That was enough for the waiter, even though he had a gun in the back of his waistband. Some fights you knew to stay out of.

The second man moved directly towards their table at the back. The dealer with the knife froze, stunned to see this mobster moving towards him. The punch was brutal, sending the guy flailing backwards past Gary, where he bounced off the wall. The second dealer's voice turned high pitched and squeaky as he started talking fast in Russian, "Hey, who the fuck are you? This is my block. I run things around here."

He didn't get any further. The mobster who had just hit his buddy slammed a fist into his gut, buckling him over. He was grabbed by the collar and marched bent over to the obvious leader of the group. Gary had figured out that much. The last guy had walked into the room while his men went to work and stood there, just inside the door watching everything unfold.

When a person at one of the other tables went to get up and leave, this third guy just raised a hand and motioned to the man to sit; the man slowly lowered himself back into his chair. Gary watched him closely, he was sure this was one of Ivan's men. He was comfortably in control and definitely had the room's attention.

This leader reached out and grabbed the dealer's hair as his man threw him on the floor. He pulled his head up and looked him in the face. "Who do you work for?" he demanded.

The dealer wasn't going to hold back, he thought the name might scare this asshole that had ruined his night out. "Bikko, I report to Bikko and he's going to be pissed when I tell him about you."

"He's going to be more pissed when I break his arm because one of the dealers he's supposed to be controlling is hassling people in bars instead of out making money like he's supposed to be." Tightening his grip on the guy's hair, the leader punched the guy in the mouth. The dealer's head swung back and forth as blood ran from the corner of his lips. "And you give up your boss' name so easily?" He hit the guy a second time and let him fall to the floor. Looking down at the dealer who was no longer listening, he added, "Who do you think Bikko reports to?"

He ignored his men dragging the two slumping dealers out of the bar as he finally made his way to the back corner. "Mr. Gary I assume?"

Gary was finally comfortable, this guy was on top of things. His close-knit crew were disciplined and followed orders.

"Yes, it is." Gary stood up and walked around the table. Chantal stood beside him. He stuck out his hand and gave Ivan's man a single firm and hard shake.

The guy wasn't wasting time, "We'll go now, I have a truck outside." He motioned towards the door and moved aside.

Gary pushed Chantal ahead of him, where he could keep her in his sights, and followed her out the door. Ivan's man was right behind. On the street the two idiots were gone. One of the crew was standing at the back of the SUV, watching the street, while the other opened the side door. Gary pushed Chantal into the truck and felt the leader get in behind him. The rest of the crew jumped in the front and they were moving in seconds.

"Where do you want to go?" Ivan's man was obviously clear on the plan and just needed the destination. Gary wasn't sure what to say. "We got off the F train so we shouldn't go there. What other line will get us back to Manhattan?"

The guy was thinking and he answered, "The B train. It's east of the F train and goes up to the top of Brooklyn then you can transfer. Okay?"

"Okay." Transferring would make it harder for anyone to follow them.

They rode in silence for a while before the mobster started asking questions, "Ivan wants to know about these men who were after you."

Gary knew that Ivan wanted to know about any men that were running around in his area without his permission. Gary was just as interested in the answers. He recounted the events.

"... then the rest of the crew came up. They must have been watching from down the street. These guys were clearly organized and had a plan. It wasn't a great plan but still they nearly carried it out." He went on to describe everything about the attackers, the van they used, the black they wore, and the fights that happened before they escaped on the run.

The SUV pulled up to the station and all three of Ivan's men got out. They escorted Gary and Chantal into the station and make sure they got on the train. Gary shook the leaders hand a second time as they parted, "I don't know your name but thank you. You're a good soldier and Ivan can be proud of the work you do."

He didn't approve of criminal activities. He tried not to get involved with people in that world, but his experiences had placed him in their paths more than once. Gary understood structure so he could appreciate the well-oiled process Ivan was clearly running. He noticed the approval in the face of Ivan's man who nodded back as the two separated.

*****

Gary was relieved to be back on the train heading home. What a night. The adrenaline crash left him beat. He kept reviewing the night's events and trying to piece things together. The attack happened. The question was why and who? That was too big a crew for a simple mugging. Why two people on the street?

Then why the hell was a professional crew that size after Chantal? She'd never been in this area before. She didn't know anybody down there. Could it be her business? Her art and photography? She wasn't rich. Neither was he, not really. He knew he might not figure it out without more information. This was nagging at him.

He couldn't believe that an innocent night at a support group meeting could turn out so bad. He wondered how Chantal was holding on. Jesus, he had probably given her a migraine instead of helping make them better.

Thinking about the end of the meeting, he tried to remember anything unusual. There were only a couple kids waiting for their mother and a hard-face man on a cell phone who had worked his way along the back row of chairs, walking out without looking back. He must not have been waiting for anyone.

And what about the black guy who Gary assumed had been helping him by fighting one of the attackers. Who was he and had he actually been trying to talk to Gary at the meeting?

He kept getting stuck on the fact that their attackers had guns they obviously weren't planning on using. It was only after the guy had lost the fight that he pulled a weapon. Gary kept coming back to what that meant. They wanted her alive. They could have done much worse but seemed to be holding back.

They'd only been seeing each other for three years. Was something from Chantal's past catching up to her? The sexy French accent fit with being a Canadian from Quebec. She told him she had come to New York to make it big. Gary was always amazed by people going all in and taking the big chance. He could relate, he's done it himself.

She did have talent. Her painting and photography were astonishing. Her work was real abstract stuff, frequently it left Gary staring at the canvas trying to figure out how it was done. She had a small apartment downtown near her gallery. He knew she kept herself in shape. She'd been training Judo since she was in her teens and ran a couple times a week. None of these things pointed to a past. She wasn't involved in a bunch of causes, or strange religions. Gary was pretty sure she was a great person and couldn't believe something was catching up to her.

No. Something entirely different was going on.

*****

Chantal was trying hard to keep awake. She leaned her head against Gary's shoulder as they rode in silence. Her body was coming down from the adrenaline and she was having a hard time making any sense of things. They had gone to a meeting, which she thought sucked, and then they tried to come home.

Everything that happened after that was insane. Why had that guy grabbed her from behind? Where did the other attackers come from? She hadn't seen a thing when she first stepped out onto the street. Thank God that Gary's martial arts training was on a whole other level compared to her Judo.

She reached up and felt the bruise forming on her neck. The guy had grabbed her pretty hard, which had only made it easier for her to flip him over her back. But dammit, it was going to look like hell tomorrow.

The funny thing was, she was more scared of the guys that showed up to help them than the attackers.

But then she supposed that had been Gary's ultimate goal.

The whole Russian theme of the night bothered her. Where in the hell did Gary know these guys from? Who in the hell was this Ivan guy he called and what was their connection? One thing was certain, the guys who came to help them were surely criminals. No doubt about it. Why would Gary know these guys in the first place?

She'd only known him three years, but had been sure about him right from the beginning. Had she been wrong? Was there a past that was coming back to haunt him? Jesus, she didn't need any more nights like this. Gary had told her his father had been posted all over the world to work in Government Embassies. Originally his father sent him to learn martial arts to deal with the bullies that confronted him at every new location. Eventually he pursued it on his own for the self-discipline and training it provided.

Chantal was sure that Gary was a stand up guy and a gentleman. She felt he couldn't have anything to do with tonight's events. Slowly, she felt herself drifting away.

Endpoint is available in paperback from Amazon.com or as an ebook from your favourite ebook retailer including Amazon, Kobo, Apple, Barnes & Noble, Sony & others.